At First
KISS

Gwyneth Bolton

KIMANI
ROMANCE

To the readers, who make real to me every day the old African proverb that states simply, I am because you are.

KIMANI PRESS™

ISBN-13: 978-0-373-86206-1

Recycling programs for this product may not exist in your area.

AT FIRST KISS

Copyright © 2011 by Gwendolyn D. Pough

www.kimanipress.com

Printed in U.S.A.

Dear Reader,

Sometimes people meet the love of their life and know right away that they have just met the person who is the other part of their soul. Sometimes people meet and become good friends before they become lovers.

And then there are other times…

Troy Singleton and Jazz Stewart didn't fall in love at first sight. They didn't even become good friends right away. *Frenemy* would be a better description for these two. They tolerate one another because their best friends are married, but that is as far as it goes. And then there's the fact he's a player and she's a serial dater. They are too much alike to ever be attracted to one another. And they can't be around one another without getting on each other's nerves. So they don't ever have to worry about hooking up or anything like that….

Or *maybe,* they are so much alike that they are really perfect for one another and it will take an act of God or something just as strong to get them to realize it.

I hope you enjoy Troy and Jazz's journey toward love as much as I enjoyed writing it!

Much love and peace,

Gwyneth

Acknowledgments

I want to acknowledge my family, because without their support I wouldn't know what love is or even be able to write about it. Special thanks to my husband, Cedric Bolton, my mom, Donna Pough, my sisters Jennifer, Cassandra, Michelle and Tashina, my nieces Ashlee and Zaria and my nephew, Michael.

Many women have shown me what true sisterhood and friendship is through the years. To my friends who have been there for me through the years and encouraged all of my early attempts at writing and listened to my dreams, thank you. I'd like to especially thank Cheryl Johnson, Elaine Richardson, Jennifer Thorington Springer, Latisha Folkes-Nwoye, Lily Marella Payne, Angelique Justin and Yolanda Hood. Smooches and triple-hold hugs to you all! I'd also like to thank my sista-authors, whose stories inspire and motivate me and whose friendship I count on. And I'd especially like to thank A. C. Arthur, Victoria Wells, Iris Bolling, Deatri King-Bey, Shelia Goss and Ann Christopher. Keep on writing those amazing stories and please keep being the wonderful women you are! Finally, I'd like to thank my sands, because they have been showing me true Delta love and sisterhood since we crossed in the spring of 1990. Thank you Kimmie, Shakira, Antoinette, Edith, Monica, Audrey, Sherita and Karen. I love you! Oo-oop!

Chapter 1

It doesn't matter if you win or lose, it's how you play the game...

Ten years earlier

So the Kappa Alpha Psi pretty boy is late. Go figure...I should have expected that from a Nupe!

Jasmine "Jazz" Stewart alternated between walking up and down the inside of the airport, checking and rechecking each luggage pickup location, and braving the cold Detroit weather outside. It had been over an hour since she had landed, and her ride was nowhere to be found. She was going to be late for her best friend's wedding rehearsal, all because some cane-swinging Kappa pretty boy—whom she had never met, but she had seen pictures of and had to admit he was too handsome for words—had no concept of time.

Her best friend, roommate and sorority sister was marrying the no-show's best friend and fraternity brother. She and Alicia were both members of Delta Sigma Theta and had pledged the Pi Iota city-wide chapter when they were sophomores in college. They were now seniors at Mount Holyoke College. From what she'd heard, Alicia's fiancé, Darren, her cousin Kendrick and the tardy Troy had all pledged Kappa at Howard several years ago, Xi chapter.

Jazz knew that her friend Alicia probably had some hopes of her and Troy hitting it off and Jazz finally becoming serious about one guy instead of dating them and dropping them, as she was prone to do. But if Troy was always this late, he wouldn't stand a chance with her. She liked her conquests to be prompt.

She glanced at the Coach watch she'd gotten a good bargain on back home at Filene's Basement in Boston. An hour and twenty-five minutes late! She had never met Mr. Troy Singleton, but from what she'd heard, he thought he was some kind of God's gift to women. He was probably used to making women wait for him. After making the mad dash to catch her flight from Boston, suffering through the two-hour turbulence-filled flight and trekking through the unreasonably long Detroit airport to get to the luggage claim spot in a timely manner so that she wouldn't keep her ride waiting, she knew for sure she wouldn't be one of the many women to fall for his charms.

She walked outside again just as a humongous gas-guzzling bright red SUV pulled up. When she saw the tall, muscular frame stepping out and walking leisurely toward the entrance to the airport, she just watched him go. The jeans and thick leather jacket he wore gave him a rugged and almost dangerous appearance. If it weren't for the air of suaveness that seemed to radiate off of him like whatever the male equivalent to a siren's call would be, he would read bad-boy-all-the-way.

She decided she hated him on sight, every six-feet-plus muscle-bound caramel-hued bit of him.

She took her luggage and rolled it over to the SUV and patiently waited for him to come back outside when he saw she wasn't in the airport waiting like a dutiful twit with nothing better to do. The brittle Detroit air almost made her want to go inside and find him, but she braved it.

Oh, the things one would endure to prove a point…

Twenty minutes later he came out talking on

his cell phone. She leaned against his car with her arms crossed in front of her. He stared at her for a moment and walked over. His expression was a mixture of perplexed and inquisitive with a slight bit of interest.

"Jasmine?" His mouth tilted slightly in a soft, sexy half smile that would probably knock the average girl off her feet.

Jazz wasn't anybody's average...

"It's Jazz. Can you open the trunk and let me put my suitcase in? We're running late. Or should I say, you're incredibly late and we're going to miss the rehearsal."

He reared his head back as if offended before narrowing his eyes. "How did you know this was my car?"

The sexy little smile was gone and she kind of missed it.

Oh. Well.

"I watched you get out of it. Can you open the trunk? And can we get in? It's cold out here." She realized that she really was starting to freeze her very ample behind off.

The cream dress slacks she wore with a cute little sweater and lightweight leather jacket, both of which were more for style than warmth, were no match for Detroit's weather. It might have been close to spring in the rest of the world, but Detroit hadn't gotten the memo yet.

"Wait a minute, you saw me get out and go inside to look for you and it didn't occur to you to try and stop me? I wasted damn near twenty minutes in there looking for you." He just stood in front of her not opening the trunk with expectation written all over his face.

He was starting to work her nerves, and the Bajan always came out in her whenever someone worked her nerves. Even though she'd left the island when she was a toddler, she was her mother's child. And Carlyne Stewart had never lost her Barbadian dialect.

She narrowed her eyes and gave her teeth a slow, lyrical suck. "C'dear…wha 'bout muh time, nuh? I wait and walk and wait and walk back and forth roun' dis godforsaken airport for I ain' no how long for yuh ta reach. We *nowhere* near even, yuh, but I ain' got time to waste belaboring the topic…" She gave him a disgusted look. "Trunk? Door?"

He pressed the automatic lock, walked over to the driver's side, got in and started up the car. She lifted her suitcase as she cursed him out in her mind and then got in the SUV.

"Woulda killed yuh to be a gentleman after havin' muh here waiting all this time, huh?" It irritated her to no end that this fool had triggered her anger so quickly and had her channeling her mother's tongue. She took a deep breath and counted to ten.

He turned up his music to some loud hip-hop and started driving, effectively ignoring her.

That was all right with Jazz. He might have been the finest guy she had ever laid eyes on, but he was also an arrogant-late-no-manners-having jerk.

Jasmine. Man what an evil—!

Troy shook his head as he made haste driving them to the small chapel where Alicia and Darren were having their wedding rehearsal. The sooner he got Ms. Jasmine Stewart out of his ride the better.

And what is with the Miss Cleo routine?

She hadn't sounded like she was from the islands at first, but then all of a sudden she went full-blown come-back-to-Jamaica on him. He didn't have the time or the patience for this crap. Not after just finding out that his parents were going to end their almost thirty-year marriage because they had supposedly "grown apart."

He chanced a glance at Jasmine. She was as pretty as her picture, even though her hair was different. Instead of the wild and free natural style from the picture, it looked like her auburn hair had been straightened somehow and it was in one of those fancy pinned-up styles with rings of curls placed strategically. She must've gotten it done like that for the wedding.

Yeah, she was gorgeous. Too bad she was such a ball buster.

And to think, he had even planned to let her be the woman he kicked it with this weekend. Everyone knew that weddings were the perfect venues for hit-it-and-quit-it hookups. He'd seen Jasmine's picture when Alicia asked him to pick up her up from the airport and he hadn't been able to get her out of his mind. He had all kinds of lines ready to woo her.

Yeah, he'd been a little late picking her up… So what? He'd gotten there. And after getting the news he'd just received, news that totally messed with his mind in ways he wasn't ready to address, she was lucky he even showed up at all.

And she played him by watching him go in the airport looking for her like a fool. Well, her loss, there would be plenty of women at the wedding looking for Mr. Right. He might not be Mr. Right, but he was for damn sure Mr. Right Now, and he wasn't going to let Jasmine ruin his plans.

Jasmine.

He *never* remembered women's names. But he couldn't seem to forget hers, or anything about her, from her pretty cinnamon face to her fierce auburn natural. And her body…

Voluptuous came to mind… Her body was definitely a throwback to the Marilyn Monroe days, when real women had curves.

He turned, looked at her and frowned.

"Keep your eyes on the road, Stud. Get us there in one piece, it's bad enough we're going to be late."

"Stud?" He couldn't help the smile that came over his face. Maybe this weekend wasn't a total loss after all...

"Yeah, if you won't call me Jazz, as I prefer, I'll just call you Stud, you know because you think you're such hot stuff, but you're really not all that. It's like a play on words... Instead of 'dud,' I'll call you 'stud.'"

He gritted his teeth. If she wasn't so fine and if he had a little less respect for women he would call her a long list of names. But instead he called her the one thing he knew she would hate.

"Cute, Jasmine. You made that up all by yourself?" He chuckled in a sarcastic manner and he could feel her bristling beside him.

The rehearsal dinner had been interesting, to say the least. Alicia must have been really trying to do the matchmaking thing because she even sat Jazz by Troy at dinner and they were paired together as bridesmaid and groomsman. If it weren't for the buffer that Troy's sister and brother-in-law provided, things wouldn't have gone well.

"So, Troy picked you up from the airport? How did that go?" Sonya asked. "I'm not supposed to be saying anything… But Alicia was kind of hoping that the two of you would hit it off."

"Nice way *not* to say anything, babe," Kendrick said with a shake of his head.

Jazz let out an exaggerated laugh. "Alicia can just forget about that…" She looked at Troy and shook her head. "It'll never happen. Never."

Troy offered a sarcastic chuckle. "Yeah, I like my women a little less high-maintenance and a lot less crazy."

Crazy? High-maintenance?

She could feel the heat rising in her neck and covering her cheeks. She did not need a repeat of her episode with Troy earlier. It was a nice upscale restaurant, and if she started cussing him out in her Bajan dialect, it probably wouldn't look good. So she smiled at him instead, a smile that probably appeared just shy of crazed.

He offered that lazy half smile, half smirk of his that she quickly came to realize worked her last good nerve and made her want to smack him. She wasn't used to these kinds of things. Guys usually didn't faze her at all. She could take them or leave them, and nine times out of ten she was leaving them. And none had never ever gotten under her skin so intensely and so quickly.

"Excuse me." She stood up and walked away from the table. She needed to go to the restroom to compose herself before she did or said something she would regret later.

After some breathing exercises and telling herself repeatedly that he was not all that, Jazz exited the restroom a newly composed woman. Until she saw Troy standing there…

"Look, before you blow up and start acting all psycho again, I just thought I'd check on you and apologize. I have no idea what I'm apologizing for, but whatever has your panties in a bunch that you perceive I am at fault for, I'm sorry."

Is my eye twitching? My eye is twitching. This— She closed her eyes, took a deep breath and willed him to be gone when she opened them.

She opened her eyes. The left one twitched. No such luck.

"Go away, Stud. No need to apologize. Clearly you can't help being just what you are, a jerk."

"I'm not going away. We need to find a way to call a truce or something. Like it or not, our best friends are about to get married and that means we are going to be seeing a lot of each other through the years. Unless of course you and Alicia grow apart after college… One can only hope…" He let his words trail off and gave her a cocky grin. "I'm kidding. I'm kidding. Lighten up, will you?"

"Alicia and I will always be close. And as for you and me running into each other in the future…

Just do your best to stay out of my way and I'll do my best to stay out of yours." She moved to walk around the arrogant man and he caught her arm.

She turned around and gave the offending hand a hard glare. He still wouldn't let go. He stepped closer until there was no semblance of personal space whatsoever.

She inhaled.

Mmm. Drakkar Noir. Nice.

"What's your problem, Jasmine? Why won't you just—" He cut himself off, and before she knew it his lips were on hers and he had engulfed her mouth, mind and all of her senses in his all-consuming grasp.

His arms locked behind her and he held her so still and so close that the only thing she could move was her mouth. And apparently her mouth wanted to move. Her tongue snaked its way into his mouth and swirled around like it had found a new playground or something.

Her heart felt like it was going to beat its way out of her chest and her toes tingled. *What the hell kind of kiss made your toes tingle?* she wondered, as she pressed closer to him, enjoying the warmth of his body heat.

We are on fire.

She sucked his tongue into her mouth and decided

to forget about her out-of-control heartbeat. He tasted too damn good.

Fire and Desire like Rick James and Teena Marie. I'm talking square biz. I'm talking lo—

She pulled her tongue, her body and her mind back at the same time and she used the hands that were trailing his massive and muscular chest to push him away. The disconnection between them was so gut-wrenching and so swift she almost fell.

It's you! You? Oh. Hell. No. Not today. Not ever!

Panting and trying to keep her heart rate from spiraling out of control, she glared at him. "What the hell do you think you're doing?"

She wiped her mouth with the back of her hand with as much disgust as someone who had literally been kissed senseless could muster. "Don't ever do that again! I do not like you. And you need to just stay away from me." She straightened her shoulders and half walked, half ran away.

Troy Singleton had taken her through a range of emotions in the space of a few hours. More emotions than any guy had ever taken her through before, and that placed him in a category all by his lonesome…

And that was just where he needed to stay, all by himself and the hell away from her. She couldn't afford to let him get too close, ever. He could never catch her slipping or she would fall…*fast*.

Troy stood in the middle of the hallway and watched as Jasmine did her breakneck dash to get away from him. The expression that a feather could knock him down came to mind. Even though he could hear a small whisper in the far nether regions of his mind whispering, *it's her, her,* he didn't want to go after her, that was for damn sure. In fact, as soon as his knees were no longer weak and his toes uncurled and stopped tingling, he was probably going to run in the opposite direction and get the hell out of that restaurant.

If he was going to live up to his boast that he would remain a bachelor until he died and then they'd have to pry his player card out of his cold, dead hands, he needed to get as far away from Jasmine Stewart as possible.

He could never allow himself to get too close to her.

Ever.

He just reminded himself how mean and evil and crazy she was. That would work, and his player status would be safe…

Chapter 2

"All the world's a stage and all the men and women merely players…"

—Shakespeare

Ten years later

"**W**ha de France yuh telling muh? Yuh mus be mad, nuh?" Stunned and increasingly livid didn't even begin to cover the feeling of dread creeping through Jazz's body. She knew she was just on the edge of losing it completely because her Bajan was coming out. Even though she had been on her mother's island home of Barbados for a couple of days now, it wasn't just being around her Barbadian kin that had made her code switch and flip on her dialect. It was the stress of losing the one person she loved more than anything in the world that had her about to snap on the puny lawyer.

The past few days had been one shock after another, starting with her mother's death.

Jazz hadn't even known that the cancer had come back. She'd been traveling a lot for work, a lot of traveling for a local television personality, anyway. And travel to and from Boston in the winter meant a lot of time spent in various airports because of delayed and canceled flights.

Airport chairs didn't invite longtime sitting, let alone comfortable sleeping. Add to that losing the only person who had faithfully had your back and a lawyer spouting nonsense about terms of inheritance in the will tied to outrageous sums of money and marriage of all things, and it was easy to see why Jazz's patience had finally run its course.

The stiff but kind of cute young lawyer seemed to sense that Jazz was on the brink of some kind of breaking point, because he moved back in his seat a little.

"Your mother has left you $500,000 with the condition that you marry in at least six months and remain married for at least two years." He nervously fidgeted with his gray tie, which perfectly matched his gray suit and did nothing to compensate for the blandness of his starched white shirt. "If you fail to do so, the money will go to your father, Clifton Williamson."

Jazz never knew her mother even had a will, let alone $500,000 to leave her. And all her life Carlyne Stewart had told her daughter never to trust no-good sorry men and to make sure she could take care of herself and never have to depend on a man.

Yet her mother had actually made it a condition of her inheritance that Jazz had to marry someone? It made no sense. None of it made sense.

Just like it didn't make sense that she was going to have to bury her mother in a couple of days. That nonsensical element was the real tipping point threatening Jazz's sanity.

Her mother was gone.

Why should anything else make sense in the world when Mom's gone?

Jazz inhaled and exhaled. She braced her back against the wooden chair for some kind of support. She closed her eyes and held them closed as she mentally counted to twenty.

When she opened them, the lawyer was still there. The will was still on the table. Her mother was still gone. And the possibility that her deadbeat—never paid one dime of child support that she knew of— father, whom she wouldn't even be able to pick out of a police lineup, would be getting a whole lot of her mother's money was taunting her brain and giving her an acute migraine.

No way would Clifton Williamson see one thin dime of her mother's hard-earned money.

No way would she get married in six months, either.

She glared at the lawyer again.

The lawyer moved even further back. "As I said, you have six months in which to get married. You're mother's will is very specific about what she wants for you. And she left you this letter to read at your leisure. She said it would explain her reasons for wanting this for you."

Reasons? Reasons? She didn't need to read the letter to get her mother's reasons. It was obvious that her mother had lost her mind in her last days. Why else would the woman who'd told her on a daily basis that she needed to be able to take care of herself and do for herself because men aren't worth a damn now be demanding that she get married?

Insanity was the *only* reasonable answer.

She reached over to take the letter off the desk and the lawyer moved back. If she weren't so irritated it would have been funny. She was tempted to really lose it and throw a serious fit that would give him a real excuse to take all the precautions he was taking. But she didn't have it in her.

She had funeral arrangements to finalize, and her

mourning wouldn't let her expend any more energy on the scared little lawyer. The only other thing she could think about was how she would make sure Clifton Williamson never spent one dime of her mother's money and how she was apparently going to have to find a husband in six months...

The island breeze and the sound of Lalah Hathaway's beautiful voice riffing and scatting like Ella Fitzgerald reincarnated made Troy feel like his impromptu trip to the Barbados Jazz festival was more than worth the wrath he was going to incur from his father/boss when he got back to Detroit. Besides the great footage the two-man camera crew was getting for his top-rated show, *Detroit Live,* he was also proving a point to his meddlesome father.

And the women...oh, the women.

Barbados in January—with its white-sand beaches, azure-blue waters, lush green foliage and breathtaking tropical flowers—all the beautiful women—both the local fare and the many who traveled from other countries to enjoy the festival— had made his trip all the more worthwhile. The bevy of beauties, the music and the atmosphere made him feel like he was in player's paradise.

"So are you really going to keep in contact with me when we get back home? Detroit is a long way from New Jersey. You're probably just on the prowl for an island fling like my girlfriends said." A high-pitched, nasal voice piped into his chill space sounding like a deep and ugly scratch on a vintage album.

Troy pulled his attention away from Lalah's melodious voice and the fine women all around him to focus on the petite cutie sitting next to him. He'd met her the night before when they were listening to Roy Ayers perform. She had been with a group of other women and stood out as the hottest one in that bunch.

But she was starting to become just a tad too clingy for Troy's tastes. And he didn't have the energy to expend making her feel secure when he'd just met her. Plus there were so many women in attendance, women more adept at the game and who knew how players play.

"Sure… We can definitely connect when we get back to the States. I travel a lot getting footage for the job. Anything that has something to do with the entertainment industry is of interest to my viewers. So, I'll definitely look you up if I'm near…" Troy struggled to remember both her name and where she was from. He hoped that his pauses hadn't clued her in.

He gave her a smile, one of his most suave displays, and added a slight wink.

She pouted, and he had to admit the little lip poking out looked sexy. He remembered what it had felt like to kiss her last night when he'd walked her back to the hotel room she shared with her girlfriends. It might not be too much energy to put in a little effort now that he remembered she was a pretty good kisser. She might have been clingy, but she was also a sexy little thing. It might be worth his while to play a little longer and see if she did other things as well as she kissed.

"Candace from New Jersey," she deadpanned as she glared at him. "My girls were so-oo right about you. You can't even remember my name after you kissed and groped me for hours last night. And I'm standing right next to you! You certainly won't be able to remember me when you get back to Detroit. You're just a player looking for some island fun!"

Troy expelled an irritated breath. She was not worth all this drama when there were so many women around. "Listen…"

"Candace!" she snapped.

Candace, that's it!

Why couldn't he remember her name? Probably because he was bad with names anyway and made it his business to use endearments whenever possible like "baby," "sweetheart" or "darling." That way he never slipped and called someone the wrong name and he didn't have to bother trying to remember them.

"Listen, Candace, I seem to remember you kissing and groping me just as much, if not more, than I did you. And I didn't hear any complaints last night." He gave her another smile, because honestly he was a lover not a fighter and all her drama was starting to become a real drain.

When she continued to give him the evil death stare, he shrugged.

It was time to cut his losses.

"You know what, why don't we just go our separate ways. I've got to connect with my crew anyway to shoot some footage of some other island hot spots for the show. And clearly you and I have very different agendas for how we want to proceed with things. So, it was nice meeting you…"

Damn, I just said her name…

"Candace!" she yelled in that horrible high-pitched voice of hers, and all the heads around them turned. She rolled her eyes, let out a huff of breath and stormed off, leaving him to face the irritated people sitting around them who had been trying to enjoy Lalah Hathaway.

Troy threw up his hands in apology. Even though he hadn't been the one to cause a scene, he shouldn't have gotten involved with the clingy woman in the first place. If he had been at the top of his game he would have pegged her for the drama-queen type as soon as he'd met her.

He could have chalked it up to his father's threats to disinherit him if he didn't settle down, leave the show and come into the boardroom. But a small voice in the back of his head had doubts.

Maybe I really am getting too old for this shit after all...

The walking dead.

That's what Jazz felt like as she walked to her airport gate dragging her carry-on bag behind her. The past few days on the beautiful island of her birth had gone by in a blur. From burying her mother, to connecting with family she hadn't seen in years, to processing the dreadful news she had gotten from her mother's lawyer, Jazz hadn't seen a good night's rest in at least a week.

The only thing she wanted to do was get back to Boston, sleep in her own bed and mourn her mother in peace. Unfortunately, when she got back to Boston, she would have to finish getting things squared away for her move and her new job in Detroit.

She was finally on her way to the big time— cohosting her own show and not just doing entertainment and girl-about-town slots on someone else's show—and her mother wasn't going to be there to enjoy it with her.

"Jasmine, is that you?"

That voice…

Good grief, not now!

Why did she have to run into the self-proclaimed playa of the decade in the middle of the Grantley Adams International Airport when she was looking and feeling like crap? And what the hell was Mr. Lover Lover doing in Barbados in the middle of January, anyway?

Troy Singleton, the jet-setting playboy, probably didn't even need a reason to be on a tropical island in the middle of the winter. He was probably just taking a spur-of-the-moment trip.

And why was he still calling her Jasmine when everyone called her Jazz? The only person that got away with calling her by her full name was her mother.

I can't stand Troy Singleton!

He walked over to her and she gave him a quick once-over. He *would* be looking all good when she looked like a hot mess. The man was tall, built like a power forward basketball player and the color of rich, deep caramel. He was, in a word or two, *hella fine*.

"It *is* you." He quickly embraced her and she

gave him the half-pat-butt-poked-out-and-away church hug.

They both let go just as quickly as they could. They couldn't get away from each other soon enough.

She had no idea what his deal was, but she knew her own reason for the quick hug all too well. Until she'd met Troy, she had never met a man she wouldn't let wine and dine her. She couldn't afford to let Troy Singleton buy her a hot dog on the street, let alone anything else at all.

She lived by the motto "Men are like buses. Miss one? Next fifteen minutes another one will be passing by." She was a serial dater and proud of it. They would never catch her slipping, and her player card was certified platinum.

"You look like death warmed over, Jasmine. What the hell happened to you?" He looked her up and down with a twisted-up expression on his face.

She glared at him and ran her hand across her head. The cute twist out she'd had when she first arrived in Barbados was long gone, and her bright auburn natural hair was now pulled into a rather funky ponytail.

And it was too darn hot for makeup, even if she had dark circles the size of tea bags under her eyes.

While her sweatsuit might not have been Juicy

Couture and was instead Hanes mix and match, it was comfortable for the long plane ride.

And who the hell was Troy Singleton to be telling her what she looked like, anyway?

She narrowed her very tired eyes. "Well, hello to you too, Stud."

He frowned at her little nickname for him.

If he refused to call her Jazz like the rest of the known and free world then she made it her business to call him anything but his name. Her favorite was variations of Stud, from Studly to Studster to Studalicious and then some.

He sighed, and she could tell the exact moment when he chose to ignore her.

"Were you at the Jazz Festival? It was amazing, wasn't it? Are you covering it for those little spots you do in Boston? Oh, wait, Alicia said you're moving to Detroit soon. Are you going to be working for my competition?"

She smirked. *If you only knew, Studdy Boy...*

"I didn't even realize the Jazz Festival was going on, I was too busy. My mom passed away and she wanted to be buried here, at home in Barbados. So I had to do that—"

He hugged her and it startled her so she stopped speaking.

"I'm so sorry to hear about your mom, Jasmine. Alicia didn't tell me that you were here burying your mother. I would have come to the funeral to pay my respects. I was here all week shooting footage for *Detroit Live*."

She cleared her throat and tried to pull away, but he held her close. "Alicia didn't know that my mom passed away. I didn't want to upset her. She's in the last stages of pregnancy with my godchild, after all."

"Our godchild," he corrected. "And she is going to be so mad at you! Alicia's going to be heated! You know she has to know everything. That's why she eavesdrops all the damn time. And when she finds out that your mom passed away and you didn't tell her…" He shook with mock fear.

"It's not like she could do anything. She can't fly this late in the pregnancy, and it would have only upset her and given her something else to worry about. I figured I'd tell her when I move there in a couple of weeks." She pulled away from him.

"You know that won't be enough to appease Alicia. She could have sent Darren, her mother, her father, my sister and Kendrick, heck, she could have even sent me to be here with you and give you moral support."

He made a show of looking at her chest, and she crossed her arm in front of her breasts.

"I'm just looking for the S on your chest, because you must think you're Superwoman or something,

Jasmine. Everyone has to lean on someone some-time."

Jazz knew he was right. But growing up the only child of a hardworking immigrant mother, she had learned early on how to fend for and count on herself. Even though Alicia Taylor-Whitman had been her best friend since college, and through her Jazz's extended family had grown immensely and she really did have people she could count on now, people that apparently included the bane of her existence, Troy Singleton, she still had a do-for-self attitude.

Great! Now her best friend was going to be pissed at her, too, just when she was finally moving to Detroit and they'd be living in the same city again for the first time since they had graduated from Mount Holyoke.

Alicia could hold a grudge like nobody's busi-ness, too. The woman had stayed separated from her husband the entire nine months of her first pregnancy because he had lied to her about their fathers arranging their marriage.

And Troy might have been boasting about how he would have been there for her, but when she moved to Detroit and took her new job, he would be singing another tune. Even her favorite playboy frenemy probably wouldn't give her the time of day once she moved to Detroit and he found out where she was going to be working.

She wouldn't have anyone…

Before she knew it a tear started working its way down her cheek, and it was soon followed by another and then another.

She tried to stop them.

She was Carlyne Stewart's strong daughter for God's sake and she did not cry in public. She hadn't cried in public during the entire week of funeral planning, the funeral or the horrid meeting with her mother's lawyer. No way was she going to break down in the middle of the Barbados airport in front of Troy Singleton of all people.

Her lip quivered.

Oh, damn. Damn it all to hell!

Troy shook his head and frowned at her before taking her ticket out of her hands and walking away.

She thought about calling after him and asking him where the hell he thought he was going with her ticket. But the tears where falling full speed now and she felt the beginnings of hiccups and snot and all kinds of things that probably wouldn't have been at all dignified. And she wanted to look at least halfway dignified when she got up the gumption to cuss Troy out. So she ran off to the restroom instead to have a nice good cry in the privacy of a stall.

* * *

Troy shook his head as he walked over to the ticket counter after telling his cameramen that he wouldn't be flying back to Detroit with them. Somebody had to look after Jasmine. The woman was clearly in no shape to look after herself. Case in point, he had never seen her looking like anything less than a million bucks and today she looked as hopeless as a penny with a hole in it.

She was still fine as all get out with her Coke-bottle figure that made a man have all kinds of thoughts and her flawless toasted-cinnamon skin.

It was just clear she hadn't slept in days and her normally funky fresh natural hairstyle of springy-corky auburn twists all over her head was now just funky.

He had to change his ticket and see her back to Boston. If he went back to Detroit and their mutual friend Alicia Taylor-Whitman found out that he wasn't there for Jasmine in her time of need, he would never hear the end of it. And since Alicia was married to his best friend Darren Whitman, and Alicia's cousin Kendrick was married to Troy's sister, Sonya, the entire family would be giving him the blues.

He paid for his ticket and paid to have her ticket upgraded to first class. No way was he flying coach, and he didn't understand how she could. He wasn't private-jet status like the Whitmans, but he couldn't remember ever flying coach in his life.

Once he'd handled the transaction he went looking for Jasmine. She wasn't where he'd left her and she wasn't sitting near the gate, so he assumed she must be in the restroom.

He stood outside of the ladies' room and waited for her to come out. About fifteen minutes later she did.

Damn! Just when he thought she couldn't possibly look any worse, she surprised him. Her eyes were bloodshot red. The tip of her nose was red as well, and her cheeks were flushed.

He handed her the new first-class ticket. "I'm going to fly back to Boston with you to make sure you get home safely—"

"You don't have to do that, Studster. I'm an adult. I think I can make it home on my own."

He cringed. Nothing irritated him more than her calling him any of her variations on Stud. He didn't know why it bothered him. He had certainly been called worse. And it wasn't like she could possibly pass judgment on him. She was as big a player as he was. And it's not like it should have mattered what Alicia's little friend thought of him anyway…

But it did.

Ever since he'd been assigned to pick her up from the airport for Alicia and Darren's wedding ten years ago, it had mattered to him what Jasmine Stewart thought of him. He had been rather late picking her up back then and they had been on the wrong foot ever since.

"That Superwoman routine is going to land your ass in the mental hospital one day, Jasmine. Let me help you, because you know Alicia is going to have a fit when she finds out. You might as well do the right thing now and then at least she won't be pissed at both of us." He grinned because he knew that would get her.

She rolled her eyes. "Alicia Taylor-Whitman is not the boss of me and neither are you, Studly." She glanced at her ticket. "First class? I can't afford first class!"

"Consider it my treat then, because I'm not flying coach."

"C'dear, black blue bloods does kill muh de way yuh does put on airs and ting." She switched back to her regular speech. "Your ass know you can fly coach." She laughed and for the first time since he'd run into her she was actually looking like her pretty self.

He shook his head.

He reminded himself that Jasmine was like family. At least she was kind of like a distant cousin that you didn't really like but tolerated during the holidays… And it was not cool to think of her in terms like *pretty*.

Although, since Troy's best friend Kendrick had married Troy's sister and Troy's other best friend Darren had married Kendrick's cousin, apparently Troy was the only one who knew it wasn't wise to hook up with women who were so close that you would never be able to get rid of them. There was no such thing as a smooth break when the ties were that connected.

And Troy *always* had to have an easy exit strategy, especially when it came to the fairer sex.

So Jasmine was *not* pretty even if she was just about the most gorgeous woman he had ever set eyes on.

"Come on, they're boarding first class, girl. Let's see if you still have jokes when you're enjoying comfy seats, better food and free drinks."

"Oh, you know I keep jokes, Studmeister."

"I know you do, Jasmine."

"Jazz."

He had no idea why she wanted to shorten such a beautiful name. And he wasn't even going to think about the fact that he never had any trouble remembering her name from the first time he'd seen her picture and been told it was his duty to pick her up from the airport. But he did like being the only one to call her "Jasmine," especially because it drove her nuts.

"Jasmine, let's go," he said as he started walking off.

"Studaroni, I'm right behind you," she said, laughing.

He chuckled. It was so easy to be around Jasmine even though she worked his nerves most times. He was glad he could help her during her time of need.

First class rocks!

Jasmine got over her mild irritation with Troy as soon as her butt touched the plush seat and the flight attendant brought her the nice hot towel to wipe her hands before giving her a glass of wine and a package of fancy macadamia nuts to snack on before takeoff.

She polished off the glass of wine and thought about how she was going to have to cut back a little in order to be able to pay Troy back for his ticket and her ticket upgrade. She knew that when he found out where she was going to be working when she moved to Detroit, he was going to regret taking the time to help her. The least she could do was give him his money back for this, because he was going to be pissed.

She yawned. All of a sudden her tiredness came

pressing down on her. It felt like a steel weight pushing her into an abyss.

"So you never did say where you're going to be working in Detroit."

"I can't say. I signed a confidentiality clause and I can't say anything until after they make the big announcement." That at least was the truth. She couldn't tell him anything even if she wanted to, not without running the risk of being sued. Never mind the fact that he would probably hightail it off the plane if he did know where she was going to be working.

"It must be big-time if they made you sign a confidentiality clause."

"I'm not saying anything."

"Fine."

She yawned again and her eyes gave in to the pressure. They closed, and her head nodded to the side and landed on his shoulder. She quickly jerked. She moved her head as soon as it touched his shoulder and she realized what had happened.

He chuckled. "You can lay your head on my shoulder, Jasmine. I won't bite you. You won't be able to put your seat back until after we reach cruising altitude and you need all the rest you can get, starting now. Those bags under your eyes look like you could have packed your clothes in them."

She shot him an evil look and he laughed even

harder before she begrudgingly smiled herself. She could have caught an attitude because of his rude way of making the offer. Or she could have even argued with him even though he was right; she did need the rest. But she wasn't stupid. She rested her head on his shoulder and let the sleep take over.

Troy stared at the sleeping beauty for a long while as her head crept from his shoulder to his chest and way too close to his heart. He resisted the urge to throw his arm around her and pull her close for all of about fifteen minutes. And he told himself that he was only doing this because Jasmine was like a third little sister, that she was just like his sister Sonya and their mutual friend Alicia. Even though he hadn't grown up with Jasmine the way he had with Sonya and Alicia, and he barely noticed that Sonya and Alicia were women, the way he couldn't help but notice that Jasmine was all woman, it was no big deal to comfort her at this moment.

He might be a player, but he wasn't a total jerk. He knew how to be a good friend, and that was all this was.

He snuggled her closer and brushed his lips across her forehead just as the very sexy flight attendant walked by to see that everyone was buckled up for takeoff. The knowing expression on her perfectly made-up face should have set off warning bells in his head. He should have been easing away from Jasmine now that she was asleep and trying to get his flirt on with the flight attendant. All of those things should have happened. And maybe one day he would be in the frame of mind to try and figure out why they didn't. The only thing he knew at that moment was that Jasmine needed him and he was going to be there for her.

Chapter 3

Player, Player…

Troy eyed Jazz's little red Mini Cooper with more than a little trepidation, and it didn't seem like he was going to get into the car anytime soon.

Since the long-term parking garage at Logan International was more than a little cold in the middle of January and she was freezing the majority of her ample behind off, Jazz needed him to man up and get his big fine behind in the car so she could warm it up, make it home and go back to sleep. The rest she'd gotten on the plane ride from Barbados had only gotten her ready for more sleep.

"Don't you have a real car instead of this match-box toy car? I'm a grown-ass man. I can't fit in this little go-cart."

Jazz rolled her eyes.

"C'dear, you and yuh won'ts and can'ts. Yuh won't fly coach. Yuh cain't ride in a little car. I startin' to think yuh even more high-maintenance dan dose Black Barbie dolls yuh date. Come nuh, get in de car and let we left dis cold place!" Jazz opened the door, got in the driver's side, popped the locks and waited for Troy to follow suit.

He glared at her and bent down to get in the car. He had to move the seat as far back as it could go and he still had to sit with his legs bent uncomfortably.

"How do you even get around in this little thing in the winter in Boston? I'm surprised it doesn't get buried in the snowdrifts. I hope you plan on getting a *real* car when you move to Detroit. This little thing isn't going to cut it."

Jazz rubbed her dashboard. "Oh, don't listen to the mean old man, Stud Buggie, you're a great car and you get mommy around just fine in any kind of weather, yes you do."

Troy winced. "Your car is named Stud Buggie?"

Her eyes widened when she realized that she had essentially named her car after Troy, since she had been calling him some version of Stud from the day she met him.

That's odd… she thought as she shook it off.

She laughed. "Don't worry, Stud. You will always be the original *Stud,* at least until you start calling me *Jazz.*" She winked at him and he glared.

"Buckle up, Studman. Time to go home." She pulled off and drove to her condo in what was now called the Mission Hill neighborhood.

Mission Hill had been a part of Roxbury when she was growing up. It was close enough to where she grew up to still feel like home. Her building was on Tremont Street and had a heated parking lot underneath. The neighborhood had a diverse mix of people and a vibrant business district as well. She realized that she would miss a lot about Beantown when she moved. But living there now that her mom was gone wasn't even an option. There were just too many memories.

Once they reached her condo she started to have second thoughts about offering up her spare bedroom/office to Troy. He couldn't get another ticket out of Boston back to Detroit until the next morning. And he insisted on staying a day or so to make sure she was okay. Since he was being so nice and everything, she didn't think it would be right to make him stay in a hotel.

So, him staying at her place was the deal.

Heaven help her!

She glanced around her sparsely decorated condo. Her mother always teased her that her lack of decorations highlighted her intense commitment phobia. She couldn't even commit to a picture. She had managed to find some pieces she could live with long term. She loved her big plush rust sofa. So what if she had changed coffee tables five times in five years and was thinking about getting rid of the current studio-style glass-top mahogany coffee table and matching end tables before she moved?

"Luckily my new gig is springing for movers and they'll be coming to pack me up next weekend, or you would be navigating your way around boxes right now. If I had to pack, I would have started last month, because it would have taken me that long with all the moaning and groaning I would be doing. I can't stand packing. We moved around from one apartment to the next entirely too much when I was a kid."

"Really?" Troy took off his jacket and took a seat on her sofa. "I lived in the same house from the time I was born until I went away to boarding school and then college."

"Across the street from Alicia's folks, right. Your mom still lives there?" She kicked off her Uggs and sat down next to him.

"No, Mom sold the house a year or two after

the divorce. She is hardly ever in Detroit any more. She's a woman of the world, traveling abroad, taking cruises, lounging in Europe, Africa, everywhere. It's like she became the person she always wanted to be when she divorced my father and that person can't sit still. I still can't believe they stayed married all those years only to divorce after Sonya and I finished college. That still trips me out." His eyes got a faraway look in them and she wondered where he went when he thought about his parents' relationship.

Jazz nibbled her lips in contemplation. "Hey, at least they managed to stay together until you guys were adults. Better that than a deadbeat for a father that you've never even met. Because my father opted out, my mother had to work all the time. So I felt like I never really had enough time with her."

Whoa, what made me share that?

She stood up. "Are you hungry, Studchickawaawaa? I could order out. I'm afraid I don't have much in the fridge. Cooking is *highly* overrated."

"We'll have to order out, because I'm not getting back in that soup can you call a car." He shuddered.

"Oh, stop complaining. Stud Buggie got us from point A to point B. And my car is really, really cute."

He chuckled. "Yeah, baby carriages are cute,

too, but you don't see grown-ass people riding in them."

"Ha, ha, ha, you're like as funny as Chris Rock. Not!" She walked into the kitchen for her folder of take-out menus. She picked up the cordless phone and noticed the flashing red light that signaled lots of messages on her answering machine. Paying extra money a month for voice mail when her phone came with a perfectly good answering machine was not her style because it took away from her Coach bag fund.

She pressed the button and took the folder to Troy. "Here, these are some of my favorite places that deliver."

"Jazz, baby girl. What's up? Why can't you call a brother every now and then? It's like that now?" The voice on the answering machine sounded familiar but she couldn't tell and she wasn't interested. By the time it reached the point of a guy calling to ask her why she hadn't called him, he was already so far off her radar, nothing could warrant the time or energy to care.

She walked back over to the answering machine and pressed delete.

"Jazzy, baby, you're breaking my heart—" Delete. She didn't recognize that voice, either, and didn't care.

"What's the matter with you, girl? You can't call

nobody?" This guy affected the voice of Martin Lawrence's infamous "Jerome, the original playa from the Himalayas" and at least got a chuckle out of her before she deleted the message.

"Jazz, why is it I had to hear from someone else that you're moving? I mean we went out a few times, and don't I even warrant a—" Delete.

She sighed as she half listened to the rest of the calls, making quick work of deleting them.

"Seriously, guys think just because you let them take you out a few times they have the right to blow up your phone and tie up your answering machine. I swear, when I move to Detroit, I'm going to stop being cheap and get an unlisted number. And I won't be giving out my main number. I need a cell phone just for this." She turned to Troy. The way he ran through the female species, he could probably understand her pain.

He was frowning.

"What's with that look? Don't tell me you don't have women blowing up your phone? And I'm sure they're calling because they gave you a little more than these guys have given me."

"And just what have those guys given you, Jasmine?"

"Ooo, that would be none of your business, Stud Bud." She laughed. "Seriously, if they're calling the phone asking why I haven't called, then they probably took me out a few times, dinner, movie, dancing, a show, nothing serious. I can usually tell after a few dates if it's going to be worth my time. And few men are worth *my* time. I'm a serial dater and proud of it. I'll date anyone a few times. And if the chemistry and connection isn't there, don't expect a call back. There are just too many men out there to waste time with Mr. Wrong—not that I'm looking for Mr. Right, no matter what my mother's stupid will demands."

She plopped down on the couch next to him.

Troy swallowed back his burning questions about all those damn messages from all those guys. Who was he to judge? His cell phone had been vibrating ever since he turned it back on when they got off of the plane, and he knew it wasn't family making all those calls. His father was probably still pissed at him. His mother couldn't be bothered. And his sister was probably good for about five of the phone calls. He made a mental note to call Sonya and let her know he was okay and back in the States. But he couldn't get Jasmine's many messages out of his mind...

He shook his head. It was not his business how many guys Jasmine had apparently enticed, entranced and evicted. He just hoped she didn't come to Detroit running those same games. He didn't know about Boston guys, but the brothers in

Detroit didn't play that. And he would hate to have to knock someone out because they came at her the wrong way after she jilted them.

He shook his head again. Where was all this I-must-protect-Jasmine stuff coming from?

Change the subject, that's all, just change the subject, he thought as he cleared his throat.

"What does you finding Mr. Right have to do with your mother's will?"

She looked stunned for a minute, as if she hadn't even realized what she had just said. She tilted her head and just looked at him. "I so-oo didn't want to bring that up. Can we just ignore it and move on?"

"Now I'm really curious. Don't tell me your mother made some crazy clause in her will that you settle down and get married or something like that. That sounds like something my demanding father would do. He just threatened to take me *out* of his will unless I settle down. And he wants me to give up my spot as the host of our media company's top-rated show, *Detroit Live,* in order to be a part of the business side of things. Can you believe that?"

"At least your dad is only making threats. Apparently, my mother managed to save $500,000 as an inheritance for me, but only if I get married in six months. And if I don't get married in six months then the money goes to my deadbeat dad. Can you believe that?"

"What? Get out of here! Your mother has my father beat. Although I wouldn't put it past my father to put some kind of marriage clause in his will. Mr. Divorced and never met a woman he didn't flirt with thinks that the only way for me to prove I've grown up and left my wild days behind is to get hitched, put on a suit and tie every day, and sit behind a desk instead of in front of the camera. He just doesn't get it."

"Why do I feel like channeling the Fresh Prince and belting out 'Parents Just Don't Understand'?" She giggled, and it was good to see her smile.

Troy shook his head. He and Jasmine were both in the entertainment business and loved music. It always tripped him out that she thought in songs just like he did sometimes. No matter what the topic, he could think of a musical reference, and Jasmine had that same knack. But there was no need to point out any similarities between them.

"Because you're a sarcastic brat and you're a nut," he offered instead, and chuckled.

"Not that I don't feel your pain, Stud Muffin, but this was kind of about *me*. My own little pity party…" She rolled her eyes in an exaggerated manner. "Recently deceased mother and actual horrendous marriage clause that threatens to ruin life as I know it no matter what I decide trumps nagging father any day. I'm just *saying…* It's not *always* about you." She laughed again.

"I'm trying to be empathetic here, Jasmine. I feel your pain."

"Yeah, *feel* it, don't *co-opt* it, Stud." She smiled and took the folder full of menus off of his lap. "Anyway, enough of that. I have six months before I either have to find one of my exes to enter into a marriage of convenience with or see the deadbeat get paid. I'm hungry now. Chinese or Mediterranean?"

Troy mulled it over. "How about pizza?"

"Pizza is always good. Toppings? I like veggies supreme."

"I like lots of meat."

"Half veggies, half meat it is," she said with a grin.

As she placed the order for their dinner, Troy couldn't help but wonder how he could help her with the situation surrounding her mother's will and why he even thought he should help her in some way.

The next morning, Jazz was awakened by the most annoying voice on the planet, followed by shaking. Before she opened her eyes, she realized that she should have locked her bedroom door. Better yet, she should have made the pest spend the night at a hotel.

"Wake up, Jasmine. We have a flight to catch."

"Man… G'long and left muh yuh hear. Leave me alone!" She pulled the cover over her head and groaned.

He had the nerve to pull the cover off of her then and she realized that he was getting a peep of her in her pink stretch lace boy shorts and camisole. She sat up and glared at him.

"Give me back the cover or die."

He gave her an appreciative once-over and laughed. "Sexy and she has fire. It might not be so bad after all being married to you. Get up and get dressed. We have a flight out to Vegas in two hours. We're getting married, Jasmine."

She jumped up out of the bed and all sense of modesty and decorum was gone. At that moment she knew she was Carlyne Stewart's daughter, because even though she had left Barbados when she was a toddler and she'd grown up in Boston, her Bajan dialect really came out with a vengeance.

She gave her teeth a long, hard suck, what the island folk called a *steups,* and placed her hand on her hip. "What de France yuh tellin' muh dis early in de morning? Yuh mus' done loss what little bit of mind yuh have, nuh?" She sucked her teeth again. "C'dear! Man left me and g'long, nuh. I does look like I crazy to you? I mus' look mad as de hatter if yuh think I'm flyin' to somebody Vegas to marry you. Gimme back mah cover, nuh?"

"Wow, you really are an island girl at heart. I like it when you do that." He had the nerve to laugh. "Anyway, hurry up and get dressed, Jasmine. We don't have all day. You don't want your deadbeat dad to get your mother's hard-earned cash, do you?"

Frowning, she sat down on the bed. She felt like Alice in Wonderland, through the damn looking glass or down the damn rabbit hole.

Things just kept getting curiouser-and-curiouser...

He sat down on the bed beside her. "Listen, the way I see it, we can help each other. You can fulfill your mother's marriage clause and I can show my father that I've settled down. That way, when we get divorced, I can say that I can't possibly ever get married again. I'd be too heartbroken. And Dad would have to back off. You'd be helping me just as much as I'd be helping you. You'd give me settled-down respectability for...how long would you want to stay married for anyway?"

"The clause gives me six months, and after that the money goes to the deadbeat. If I get married in six months and remain married two years or more I can keep the money. If I remain married less than two years but more than six months half of the money goes to me and half goes to a charity for single mothers and their children, less than six months and half goes to the deadbeat, half to the charity and none to me. She has me over a barrel because I don't want even half of her hard-earned money to go to him. But I wouldn't mind sharing it with the charity."

He sighed. "Then marry me, Jasmine. We can last two years and then you can still donate part of the money to the charity and keep the rest. You're moving to Detroit anyway. It would take you more than six months to find a husband in a new city. I'm already there. Marry me." He stood up and held out his hand.

"We'd have to live together for two years, Studalicious. We'd kill each other in two months." She chuckled softy as she let herself think about what it would be like to be married to Troy. Did she even dare?

"No, we wouldn't. We could do this. It's the best solution for both our problems." He laughed. "And I never thought I'd be getting married, let alone begging a woman to be my wife. Just get dressed already. The car will be here in an hour."

"What car?"

"The airport service. I told you I'm not getting back in that little soapbox car of yours again. We can get breakfast in the airport before we take off."

She mulled it over. It seemed like the answer to all her problems. She looked at Troy.

Fine didn't even begin to describe the tall drink of water standing in her bedroom exuding a heady cocktail of confidence, arrogance and just-do-the-damn-thing sexiness.

Being married to him would be the most difficult thing she had ever done. Because—as much as she loved to irritate him and work his last nerve—he had the power to push her buttons in ways that no man ever had. And if she married him and he was as angry as she knew he would be when he found out all about her new job in Detroit, it would be as good as giving her father half of the money. But at least the charity would get the other half…

Troy would want a divorce for sure.

But maybe, just maybe he would be understanding and would keep to their deal anyway.

"Are you sure about this, Stud? I mean, it would be two years where we would have to live together, and I'm not sure how your many women would feel about that."

"They wouldn't matter. I wouldn't see other women while we were married, Jasmine. And I would hope that you'd be able to ward off your many admirers for two years. We'd have to keep up appearances if it's going to fool my dad. And if you are all over Detroit serial dating then he's going to think I'm cuckolded and can't control my woman." He did that cocky half smile, half smirk thing of his and she willed the goose bumps not to pop up all over her body.

"Yeah, well, I hope you remember appearances when your women keep throwing themselves at your feet, Studman. I don't want to look like the poor little woman whose man can't keep it in his pants."

He laughed. "Fine, then get dressed. Throw some stuff in a bag and let's do this." He was still standing there holding out his hand. "Let's go to Vegas and get married."

She stood up and shook his hand. Her knees almost went weak and she felt a strange tingling in the pit of her stomach. Touching him felt too nice to be right, and she let out a long sigh.

Goose bumps popped all up and down her arms as she looked into his serious and sensuous eyes. She suddenly felt an overwhelming desire to be honest with him.

"Before we do this I should tell you about my new job, Troy."

"Didn't you sign a confidentiality clause?"

"Yes, but—"

"But nothing. You better keep that information to yourself. I can't promise I wouldn't break the story on *Detroit Live* before you even moved to Detroit. If it's entertainment news in my city, people expect Troy Singleton to be on it. I don't want to betray your trust. So, I'm willing to find out with the rest of Detroit. I just want you to know, if our competition has hired you to host some show meant to compete with *Detroit Live,* you being married to me isn't going to stop me from slaughtering you in the ratings, Jasmine."

Her shoulders reared back and she sucked her teeth with a steups that would have made any Bajan proud. "Well all right den! Yuh mus' know better dan me. G'long and we'll see who gwan reign supreme once I get to Detroit. Yuh wan' a wife. Yuh gone get a wife. But don' be mad when yuh find out what dis wife come to Detroit to do, yuh hear?"

He laughed. "I love it when you do that. Hurry up and get ready, girl. The car will be here in forty minutes." He walked out and she sighed.

She hoped she was doing the right thing, because it could all blow up in her face. And she wasn't just thinking about what could happen when Troy found out about her new job.

No, she was thinking about what could happen to her after being married to a man that funny and fine and caring and almost perfect for her for two years.

Could her heart take such a test in temptation?

Troy stared at Jasmine and wondered why he wasn't wondering if he was doing the right thing.

His resolve to marry her had gotten stronger and stronger from the moment he thought of the idea as he lay awake the night before in her guest bedroom, to the time it took him to make the arrangements that morning while she slept, to the limo ride from her house, to the airplane ride to Vegas and finally the limo to the hotel.

And now that he was standing across from her in the small wedding chapel just off the Vegas Strip, he felt an even firmer resolve.

This was the right thing to do.

Even the sure and steady beat of his heart and the spreading warmth in his chest that he had decided to ignore told him he was doing the right thing.

And then the funniest thing happened. The entire time they listened to the minister and they repeated their vows he told himself that he would only give her a peck on the lips or cheek when it came time to kiss the bride.

It wasn't a *real* marriage, after all.

There was no need to get it twisted.

It was just a marriage of convenience so that she could get her inheritance and he could get his father off his back for a little while.

But then he looked at her with her pretty face, wearing just enough makeup to bring out the glow in her cinnamon-toasted skin and just enough lipstick to make him want to smudge it or try and see how much of it he could kiss off of those luscious lips. And he remembered the first time he'd been crazy enough to taunt fate and kiss her. Her mouth was like the sweetest ambrosia.

He also remembered what her body looked like in those lacy undergarments she slept in and the way his heart and other parts of him sprung awake when she touched his hand.

Later he might be able to rationalize that all of those things and the thought of really getting married must have been the reason why he turned crazy and kissed her.

But at that moment, when the minister said, "You may now kiss your bride," all Troy could think was *mine*.

He pulled her into his arms and covered her mouth with great speed. Her lips felt plush and were sweeter than anything he'd ever tasted. Her lips parted in shock and he used that opening to allow his tongue to devour her even more.

He let his arms feel her all over and caress her in ways that he knew he would always remember and would be hard pressed to not want to do more of, over and over again.

She felt good in his arms. She felt right. Her pert and proud breasts pressed against him and he could almost swear he felt her nipples poking him. He kept kissing her until she was suddenly kissing him back. Her hands reached up to his shoulders and pulled him closer.

She moaned, and he knew he was in trouble.

Jazz relished the feel of Troy's strong, steely arms

holding her; his fever-inducing hands trailed over her body and turned her insides into a molten pool of lust. Her tongue tangled with his as if it didn't know any better, as if it weren't attached to her brain and her heart, both of which seemed to be willing to chance whatever kind of wild ride Troy Singleton was taking her on.

And her hands?

The traitorous little things might just as well be tearing down the wall she had built over the years to protect her heart and keep herself safe from just this kind of thing, the way they were roaming all over Troy's big, strong, sexy body.

She sucked his lower lip and nipped it.

Mmm…tastes delicious…so damn good!

She groaned.

Oh, this has to stop. But…wow, I had no idea a tongue could even do that! I wonder what else he can do with that tongue.

Oh. My. God. Okay. Enough.

She pulled her mouth away from his with much effort. It took everything in her not to go back for seconds. The husky minister was grinning up a storm and his petite and perky assistant was smiling as well.

"Nothing warms my heart more than seeing two people in love. May God bless your union and you keep that love and passion for one another through the years," the minister said with all the force of a decree.

Jazz stared up at the man who spoke the words. It should have felt like a curse instead of a blessing. The minister's words should have sent her running from the chapel. Instead all she could do was look at Troy…look at her *husband* and whisper, "That *cannot* ever happen again."

Troy took a deep breath and let it out. He closed his eyes and shook his head like he was trying to shake off a fog. When he opened them he ran his hand down his face.

All she could think was, finally one of us is smart enough to show some signs of regret. Because goodness knows even though she had mustered up the strength to whisper her feigned indignation, she was having a hard time calling forth anything like regret or holding back the desire to kiss him again and then some.

He let out a sigh. "We'll see, Jasmine."

What the hell? We'll see?

She knew she must have looked stunned. But she couldn't for the life of her figure out what to say. He had lost his mind and she apparently wasn't far behind.

She took a deep breath, all the while keeping eye contact with his deep stare.

She smiled. "I guess I can't call you Stud anymore,

huh?" She licked her lips, savoring the taste of him that still lingered. "I'll have to upgrade you now."

"Yeah?" He laughed. "What's higher than number one?"

She reached up and touched his cheek. "You just moved from 'Stud' to 'Hubby,' or any form of that I might come up with. And I'm already thinking of a million ways to say it. Unless, of course, you'd like to start calling me Jazz as a wedding present."

He shook his head. "Sorry, no can do, Jasmine."

"Well, let's go back to the hotel, then, Hubby."

Chapter 4

Play on, player…

The move to Detroit was almost uneventful. Jazz had to cancel the lease on the apartment she was going to rent, because she was moving into Troy's home for appearances' sake. But she still questioned her own sanity about her decisions, everything from her decision to marry him to her decision to move in with him after he pretty much kissed her senseless on their wedding day.

Luckily they made it back from Vegas without doing anything else that could be considered crazy and reckless. As soon as they left the chapel they went back to the suite and retreated to their separate bedrooms.

She didn't know about Troy, but she spent the night tossing and turning in heated, pent-up, passionate frustration. It was all she could do not to get up, knock on his door and offer him a wedding night he wouldn't soon forget.

And now she was in his home…

After he picked her up from the airport and they grabbed a bite to eat, they were seated in his living room.

He lived in a Colonial Revival-style home in the Indian Village Historic District on the east side of Detroit. The neighborhood was quaint, and many of the older early-twentieth century homes had been renovated; like Troy's, they were all well kept. A nice comfy-homey feeling overcame her as soon as they drove into the neighborhood, and it didn't subside once they entered Troy's house. He had the kind of home that people raised families in, and it went against every idea she had about him being a die-hard bachelor.

Compared to her sparsely decorated condo, Troy's place looked like it had been professionally decorated. He clearly loved to surround himself with style and beauty. Everything had that well-put-together look, from the chic Italian leather furniture in the living room to the carefully selected artwork that graced the walls. The only thing that looked strangely out of place was this ugly brown plaid reclining chair that sat right in front of the television. When she asked him about it, he claimed it was his man chair and she wasn't allowed to sit on it without permission.

Whatever.

Other than the eyesore of a chair, she immediately felt like she could actually live there for a while. That is, if Troy didn't ask for a divorce when he found out about her job.

The rest of her clothing would arrive sometime during the week and the movers would be moving what little furniture she'd decided to keep to a storage unit.

The only thing she and Troy had yet to figure out was the sleeping arrangements, and she wondered how she could tactfully bring that up.

"So…I haven't really thanked you for doing this… you know…marrying me and everything. I really want to thank you for that."

Yes, that's it. Start out with being nice… That's a good segue to letting him know that there won't be any repeats of that kiss and certainly no getting-of-the-goodies.

"You want to thank me?" His deep voice held a suggestive tone, and she frowned.

Leave it to Troy to take her from nice and friendly

to evil and attitudinal in less than sixty seconds flat. She glared at him and twisted her lips to the side.

He chuckled. "What? One minute you want to thank me and the next you're looking at me like you want to kill me." He smiled. "You don't have to thank me, Jasmine. You're helping me, too. We do have to decide when we're going to tell people. I'm pretty sure that Alicia and Darren are going to be upset when they find out we got married without telling anyone. And they won't have anything on how my parents and my sister and brother-in-law are going to react. When do you want to tell everyone?"

She sighed.

Yet another layer of complication...

"I don't know, Troy. I really hate the thought of lying to our friends and making them think we're married."

"Umm...hello...we *are* married." He held up his hand and pulled up hers to show their platinum wedding bands. His was a wide band and hers was a dainty thin one.

"And before I forget, you should wear this, too, or no one in my family will believe that we are for real."

He pulled a ring out of his pocket, a beautiful ring.

The antique art deco-style engagement ring was platinum with sapphires and had a bejeweled vaulted frame centered with a humongous bezel-set round diamond surrounded by eight silhouette spheres that were also bezel-set; they were interspersed with channel-set French-cut baguette sapphires.

"This was passed down to me from my grandmother, and it's supposed—"

"It's supposed to go to your *wife!* Oh, my God, Troy, I can't take this. It's gorgeous. It's beautiful. It's absolutely stunning and there is no way I can take this. We have the wedding bands and that should be enough."

He took her hand and slid the ring on. It was a perfect fit. Her thin wedding band nestled perfectly against it and didn't take away from the beauty of the ring.

She couldn't help herself as she gazed at it like it was her long-lost friend. She had to say it. "I love it."

He laughed. "Great! Wear it."

She couldn't take her eyes off it. It was perfect and the bling was blinding. Finally she just mumbled. "Well…if you force me…I guess I'll have to wear it." She didn't even bother trying to feign being put out by it. It wasn't a hardship to have to rock a rock like that.

"Now, back to how you want to tell people. I've stayed away from folks all last week because I knew you wanted to make the announcement together and I knew they would ask about my ring—"

"You've been wearing your ring all week?"

"Umm…yeah… Haven't you been wearing yours?"

"Well, yeah, but I don't really have anyone in Boston that I'm that tight with that I can't just tell to mind their own business. You could have just taken the ring off and gone on about your business."

His phone rang and he answered it. From the change in the pitch of his voice it was clearly a woman.

All of a sudden she felt herself getting a little heated. She had never been one to get overly possessive about any guy. But then she had never been married to one before.

She folded her arms across her chest and narrowed her eyes as she listened to him.

"So, that's not going to be able to work. I recently got married and… Well, we haven't made any announcements… A week ago… I know I was single two weeks ago before I went to Barbados… Listen… uhh…Sheila, I knew that. I know who I'm talking to… Sheila, right…listen, I certainly don't want to hurt anyone's feelings, especially yours. But I'm not going to disrespect my wife or my marriage. So, you'll have to stop calling me."

There was some high-pitched screaming, yelling

and cursing that Jazz could hear just sitting next to him. She wanted to tell him to just hang up, but she bit her tongue for the moment.

A soon as he hung up the phone it rang again. He gave her an apologetic stare and she sucked her teeth.

"You need to tell them heffas you're married now. In fact, you need to change the number, like yesterday." She crossed her arms across her chest and huffed.

"I will. I'll change the number as soon as I get off the phone." He answered it. "Hello… Hey, what's up, Darren?"

When he hung up the phone he had a big grin on his face. "Alicia had the baby. Our goddaughter has come into the world. I know you want to go the hospital."

"You know I do!"

Her cell phone rang and she answered it. "Hey, Darren. Yes, I'm in Detroit. Of course I'm coming to the hospital. I was there for your firstborn and your second. There's no way I'll miss the third, especially not when you're finally making me the god-mommy. I'll see you guys in a few."

"So it looks like at least two of our friends are about to find out we're married." Troy grinned and then he frowned. "I just hope that Alicia doesn't get mad and decide that we can't be the godparents of this little girl."

Jazz frowned, too. She hadn't even seen the little girl yet and she was already in love with her. She absolutely adored Alicia's little boys. She loved Alicia's children as if they were her own. She didn't have a sister, and Alicia was the closest thing she'd ever had to one. Those kids were family to her no matter what.

"Oh, no. She had better not. She let your sister Sonya and Kendrick be the godparents of little Darren Jr. nine years ago."

"Well, Darren and Alicia did get together after being bridesmaid and groomsman at Sonya and Kendrick's wedding," Troy reasoned.

"I know and I gave them that one—" Jazz agreed, even though back then she had been highly upset about that decision, since she had been the one who had made the trip to the drugstore to buy all those pregnancy tests and she had been the one to tell Alicia that she might be pregnant. Little DJ should have been her godson.

But she was over it…really she was…

"Yeah, but letting Flex Towns and Sweet Dee be the godparents of little Kyle Jonathan, that was just wrong!" Troy said with a hint of disgust.

"To be fair, Alicia was always a big fan of Sweet Dee when she was a rapper and then when Dee and

Flex had little Fredrick Towns IV at around the same time that Alicia and Darren had Kyle and they asked Alicia and Darren to be the godparents to their child because Alicia's meddling brought them together a little sooner—" Jazz started to reason.

"Whatever, Kyle should have been our godson!" Troy chuckled. "I claim them all anyway."

"Me, too!" Jazz laughed, not at all surprised that she and Troy were so much alike when it came to their friends' adorable kids. "And I think it's wonderful that my little godbaby waited for me to get to town. Let's hurry up. I can't wait to see her."

When they got to the hospital, they found the waiting room filled with Alicia and Darren's family. Alicia's parents were too busy scolding Jazz for not telling anyone that her mother had passed away so that one of them could have gone with her to the funeral to notice that she had come in with Troy.

It took about thirty minutes before someone realized that something was going on between Jazz and Troy.

In hindsight, she realized that the two of them weren't sniping at each other, cracking jokes or using song lyrics to make subtle digs at one another the way they normally did whenever they were around one another. The silence between them alone was a big glaring warning sign.

But the clear giveaway had to be the wedding rings, and that announcement was thanks to Troy's sister, Sonya. It was actually kind of shocking that it took her so long to notice the bling.

"Oh, my goodness," Sonya shrieked at the top of her lungs. "You both have on wedding rings and that…" She grabbed Jazz's hand. "That is my grandmother's engagement ring. How did you… Oh. My. God. Troy and Jazz are married!"

It felt as if everyone had been dancing and partying and the record scratched, because the entire room went still and then everyone was talking at once.

"Yes, we got married. Surprise!" Jazz tried to make light of it. Then, thankfully, Darren's parents came out of Alicia's room.

Jazz grabbed Troy's hand and pulled him with her. "Well, we'll answer all of your questions when we get back. We have to go and see our sweet goddaughter now."

They barely escaped from one room full of questioning people to another that held only two people and a newborn baby girl but offered no reprieve from the questions.

"Jazz, I am very salty with you right now. Why didn't you let us know that your mother died? I had to hear it from Sonya, who heard it from Troy."

Jazz glared at Troy.

"I'm sorry, Alicia, I didn't want to put any extra stress on you during the last stages of pregnancy while you were carrying my goddaughter. And look at her! She's absolutely gorgeous. You're going to have to buy a shotgun, Darren." She reached over and took the baby from Alicia's arms.

The little angel had a headful of glossy, black curly hair and alert hazel eyes like her mother's. It was hard to tell if she would take after Darren's honey complexion or Alicia's milk chocolate skin tone, since she was looking kind of red at the moment.

"She's beautiful. What are you guys going to name her?"

Alicia laughed. "Darren wants to name her Alicia, but there can be only one."

Darren chuckled. "And we thank God for that."

Alicia glared at her husband in feigned outrage, but love was clearly written all over her face. "So we decided to name her Ashley."

"Hey, little Ashley. Hey, precious. It's your god-mommy." Jazz cooed at the little darling as she held her, and she felt a stirring that she had never felt when she held babies before. She wanted her own little bundle to hold and rock and coo to.

"And your god-daddy is here, too, little Ashley," Troy chimed in.

Jazz looked at Troy and could tell he was beyond

smitten with the little girl already, as was she. She decided to let him hold her for a bit, since they would have to share this little girl for the rest of their lives.

"Well, Alicia, you're going to find this out anyway, and I want you to hear it from me." Jazz held up her had. "Troy and I are married. We got married in Vegas last week. You know that he and I met up when we were both coming back from Barbados and well…" She affected her best Shug Avery from *The Color Purple*. "I's married now. I say I's married now."

Alicia's jaw dropped but no words came out. Jazz had never seen her friend speechless, ever. That had to be some kind of unnatural occurrence…a lot like Jazz actually getting married. She supposed if anything would shock her friend speechless that would be it.

"Say what? Get out of here. What happened to they-will-have-to-rip-my-player-card-from-my-cold-dead-hands and I-will-never-fall-victim-to-the-ball-and-chain?" Darren seemed shocked, too. But at least he found his voice enough to ask Troy questions.

Troy laughed, totally absorbed in little Ashley's world. "Things just happen, man. What can I say?"

"Give me my baby." Alicia had clearly found her voice and she didn't sound very happy. "I can't believe you got married without telling me, Jazz. That is just too much. We are supposed to be girls. I tell you everything. Everything."

Troy glared at Jazz. She could tell that he knew what might come next if they didn't appease Alicia quickly…

Godparent honors were going bye-bye.

"You're right to be upset, Alicia. I'm a horrible person and an even worse friend. Charge my mind, not my heart. Since my mother passed, I have been out of it. Thank God for Troy. Having him has literally saved me. I don't know what I would have done without him these past few weeks. He's been my rock. And I have you and your attempt at matchmaking to thank for sending this wonderful man into my life. If only I had known back then that I was meeting the only man I would ever trust enough to marry."

Alicia's face brightened just a little as she rocked little Ashley in her arms. The only thing that could soothe her know-it-all friend was the perfectly pitched I-was-wrong-and-you-were-right speech.

"I was right, wasn't I?" Alicia glowed, and it was more that that new-mother glow at work. "You two are perfect for each other. It's about time you realized what I've known all along."

"That's because you're so brilliant and the rest of us are a little slow," Troy added.

Jazz smiled at him.

Good addition, Hubster!

"Mmmm… I don't know about this. What happened exactly? Why did the two of you decide to get married instead of, oh, I don't know, dating for a minute to see if you were really compatible?" Darren didn't seem to be buying their story.

Jazz froze. Since when did Darren become all relationship savvy and aware? If he kept talking their flattery wouldn't do a thing to appease Alicia. She had to think of a save…

Troy cleared his throat. "You know, Darren, there just comes a time when you have to man up. Seeing her again in the airport of all places, so similar to the place we first met… It just felt like déjà vu. Only this time I was prepared for her, you know." He gazed into her eyes and she tried not to laugh.

"And I knew you and Kendrick would think I was crazy, but I knew we had to elope right then." Troy shook his head. "Yeah, I never thought I'd be doing it this soon. But I'm a grown man now." He placed his arms around Jazz and pulled her close. "And I have a winner this time. And all I knew was I didn't want her for a one-night stand, or hit it and quit it, or even a girlfriend. I wanted her to be my wife."

It was all Jazz could do not to roll her eyes. Troy's words would have been perfect if he hadn't paraphrased and stolen them from a Raheem

DeVaughn song… He had better hope that neither Alicia nor Darren recognized the pieces of the lyrics that he had just copied.

"Aww, that's so sweet," Alicia said with a sigh. "What about you, Jazz? What made you decide to marry Troy? You always said he was irritating and made you sick. And I quote, 'Troy Singleton is a wanna-be player with absolutely zero game.' And—"

"Yeah, well, clearly it was a case of protesting too much." Jazz had to cut Alicia off. There was no need for Troy to hear *every* negative thing she ever said about him, especially when he'd been so nice and his kiss had been so intoxicating and his game was so-oo not a zero. It was more like one plus seven zeroes for sure…

"Well, what made you realize that you wanted to marry him so quickly?"

"I…ummm… Well, you know what…" Jazz all of a sudden wasn't so irritated at Troy resorting to R&B to answer the Whitmans' probing questions. They were some nosy-ass-put-you-on-the-spot-people for sure. Jazz had to resort to R&B herself to get Alicia off her back.

Jazz sighed. "I was just at the point in my life where I was just tired of playing games. I thought… it's time to settle down. Maybe buy a house or something like that… Have some kids. Live life, you know? Maybe even change my last name… I've been a superwoman for so long… That I was just ready to become his wife… Plus, I figured I'm not going anywhere and he's not going anywhere and love has taken over, so we might as well make it official…" She felt Troy squeeze her shoulder tightly so she figured she was going too far. She reined it back in.

"Anyway, girl, we need to go ahead and let some other folks get in here to see you. I'll be back and you know I'll be over as soon as you're released to spend time with Ashley, Kyle and DJ."

She and Troy left the hospital after saying goodbye to everyone. And as soon as they exited the door, Troy frowned at her.

"Lil' Mo's '4 Ever,' really? Is that the best you could do? You're lucky they didn't pick up on your little remix." He shook his head in mock disgust.

"Oh, really? I know you're not talking because Raheem DeVaughn called and he said he'd like the lyrics to 'My Wife' back."

They both started laughing when they realized that they'd each resorted to the thing they used to do to insult each other to offer their highly questionable answers to Alicia and Darren's questions.

"Maybe Alicia was right," Troy mused.

"Oh, goodness, we only said that to appease her so she wouldn't cancel their offer to let us be adorable little Ashley's godparents." Jazz rolled her eyes. "Please don't let this become a habit and start saying this all the time now. Right about what?"

"Maybe we are perfect for one another after all…."

She swallowed. She had no idea what to say to that.

Chapter 5

Foreplay…

Jazz continued to mull over the words Troy had spoken as they left the hospital. She also thought about the kiss they'd shared on their wedding day and the one they had shared ten years earlier. The one that had probably started it all… She wondered if Troy really meant all the little innuendos he'd been spouting these past couple of weeks.

When she thought about how his lips felt, so firm, so soft, so amazing, and when she thought about how steadfast he'd been since she ran into him in the Barbados airport, she honestly didn't think she would have been able to cope with the loss of her mother without him. Forget the will, the marriage clause and their marriage of convenience.

She was beginning to count on him, and she was even opening up to him.

That was a big problem.

"So, I believe we have some sleeping arrangements to work out."

Startled, Jazz jumped. She sucked her teeth and broke into her patois. "Wa de France, yuh creepin' up pun me like you dun loss you mind. Yuh try tuh give me a heart attack?"

He laughed. "Wooo, I love it when you go all Bajan on me. Did you visit there a lot when you were younger?"

"No. This is all Carlyne Stewart's doing. She didn't have a thick accent, but when she got mad, man, watch out, yuh here. She'd cuss yuh real real bad, nuh." Jazz started laughing. It was the first time since burying her mother that she could remember her and not have her chest feel like it was about to cave in.

Troy put his arms around her. "You miss her a lot, don't you?" He wrapped her up so close to him she could smell his deep and spicy sandalwood cologne.

The smell made her think of strength and shelter from any kind of storm, real or imagined. It made her lean into him and inhale. His pectorals and abs felt muscular and sturdy beneath his shirt as she nodded her head in response to his question.

"I still can't believe she's really gone. I don't have anyone now."

His hold tightened. "That's not true, Jasmine. You have Alicia, Darren, the kids—our beautiful new goddaughter…and…me. You have me, Jasmine."

He bent down and brushed his lips across her forehead. Her insides turned to jelly. She moved her head from his chest and gazed up at him.

Suddenly, it didn't matter that he'd gone from the guy she couldn't stand to the guy she couldn't get enough of in such a short period of time. It didn't matter that she wasn't sure how he was going to react when he found out about her job. It didn't even matter that he had somehow broken through her shield of protection and was working his way into her heart.

The only thing that mattered was at that moment she wasn't afraid of what she was feeling for him. She wanted to embrace it.

He bent his head down and captured her lips with his. The charge from the initial contact brought her up on her toes searching for more. She opened her mouth and let her tongue circle its way into his mouth. She nipped and nibbled, sipped and suckled, and she couldn't get enough. She reached up and placed her arms around his shoulders, his big, buff shoulders.

She knew this was going to happen.

From the first time he'd kissed her all those years ago, she'd known they were barreling headfirst into this uncharted and dangerous territory. But damn if she wasn't tired of running from it.

She pulled her lips away and immediately missed Troy's tantalizing kisses.

"What are we doing, Hubby? We're not supposed to be doing this."

"Says who? We're two consenting adults and you're *my wife*."

"Yes…there's that…" She licked her lips, savoring the taste of him.

"Can you honestly say that you've never thought about how it would be between us?" He nipped her bottom lip and sent a thrilling electric charge through her stomach that made her thighs quiver.

She wanted Troy Singleton. She wanted him bad.

Still, she couldn't help but wonder where all of this pent-up passion was coming from. How did he sneak past her defenses?

"Tell the truth, Jasmine. Our first kiss and the kiss on our wedding day last week were amazing. I know you felt it then. I know you feel it now." He kissed her again as if trying to prove his point.

His lips started out smooth and silky, with brushes of tenderness that felt almost feather-soft. Each touch of his succulent mouth on hers sent tiny charges through her, willing her to open for him.

As soon as she did, his tongue seized the moment and circled hers with almost dizzying speed and focused determination. It went under and over and under and over, flicking the roof of her mouth with each trip and creating an almost kinetic energy in its wake. His hands cupped her behind and he squeezed, pulling her closer to him, close enough for her to feel his desire for her.

Each time he kissed her it seemed to build on the first time. Each time he kissed her she could no longer hide the fact that something vital had changed between them at first kiss and there never was any going back. She had fooled herself into thinking she could run from it.

Good morning, heartache... The only man who could spark any kind of emotion in her, any level of caring, had pulled her card. When he left her, she would be devastated. But she intended to make some great memories before that happened.

She pressed herself closer to him, wanting to merge with him in every way possible. Taking a deep breath, she glanced up at him.

"After the kiss on our wedding day, we said we wouldn't muddy the waters, that we wouldn't push this. Hubster, this could very well change everything." She couldn't help the sexy, playful, flirty smile that crossed her lips, and damned if she could prevent the "come hither" in her gaze. She couldn't turn off her desire for Troy if she wanted to, and she didn't want to.

She wanted to do so many other things…

His eyes became even more hooded and he nibbled her lips again. "Sometimes change is good. I want you, Jasmine. *Bad.* I think we can have all the benefits of our marriage and still remain friends if you decide you want to end this in two years."

She laughed, and the throaty, sexy laugh she usually saved for when she was trying to slay a brother with her sexiness came out.

She really couldn't turn *it* off. The sex kitten refused to be caged.

"But we aren't friends, Hubby. We're *frenemies,*" she corrected. "And what do you mean if I decide to end this in two years? That's what we agreed on, right?"

"Yes. That's what we agreed on." He kissed her again, and all of her questions faded to the background.

His kiss deepened and she decided to just let go. She could think about all of the drawbacks to muddying the water and worry about how Troy might react when he found out about her new job later.

Right now, she wanted to feel him. She wanted to experience what she had been denying herself ever since he'd kissed her senseless ten years ago.

She reached her hands up and pulled open his shirt. Buttons went flying everywhere, but she couldn't focus on them. All she could focus on was the fact that the stupid undershirt was in her way and she couldn't touch his skin.

She wanted skin to skin.

He took a step back, pulled off the ruined shirt and took off his undershirt. "If you don't want me to ruin that pretty little blouse the way you ruined my shirt, I suggest you start stripping. Now."

She laughed again, and she slowly and seductively undressed. "Sorry about the shirt. I don't know what came over me. Must be all your sexiness driving me crazy."

"I've been known to do that…" He took off his pants and her eyes roamed from his firm calves to his muscular thighs and stopped at his black boxer briefs to admire the very full package he sported. It was standing at attention and ready to go.

She made quick work of the rest of her clothing, stopping at her black lace boy shorts and matching camisole. She eyed his boxer briefs again and then did a quick spin.

"Beautiful," Troy said as he pulled her, midspin, into his arms. He lifted her up, planted her on his reclining "man chair" and spread her legs so that they each cradled an arm as he kneeled in front of her. He slid off her boy shorts and kissed his way from her toes to her upper thigh.

She took a sharp intake of breath when his kisses centered on the most intimate kiss of all and his tongue and lips explored her slick wet folds with a focused intensity aimed at making her explode.

She threw her head back when—after what seemed like a lifetime of his fierce tongue action and her squirming, squealing, sliding and squeezing— the most intense orgasm ripped through her and caused her to scream his name at the top of her lungs.

He continued to lick and suck until another smaller aftershock of an orgasm made her shake and sigh. She was so busy basking in the afterglow that she barely noticed when the recliner went back and he covered her body with his and entered her in one smooth sure motion.

The overwhelming sense of being filled to overflowing caused her to open her eyes. His mouth swooped down and covered hers, sharing her taste with her.

His tongue probed her mouth as deftly as his sex probed hers. Her hips lifted and she moved her legs from the armrests, placing them around his back in an effort to feel even more of him. The chair rocked back and forth along with them, creating a soothing lull that seemed to go against the powerful passion of their thrusts.

"My. God. Jasmine. You don't know how long I've waited to feel you like this."

She let her tongue trail his chest and enjoyed the salty taste of him.

"It's only been a little over a week since we've been married, Hubby. I'm sure you've waited longer…"

He nipped her nipple through the black lace of her camisole. "Next time all of this has to go." His thrusts picked up an even stronger pace and soon, in addition to rocking, the chair was squeaking and thumping.

"You feel so damn good. I knew you'd feel this good the first time I laid eyes on your picture."

Something inside of her chest thawed and she struggled to maintain her protective shield. She pulled his face to hers and kissed him hard as she met his thrusts with her own.

"You don't have to run game. Game recognize game, player." She chuckled nervously as she realized she was running the biggest game of them all, trying to convince him and herself that she hadn't felt something for him from the first moment she'd laid eyes on him as well.

"This is not a game, Jasmine. This as real as it gets and as real as it's ever been. Can you handle it?"

An orgasm ripped through her and she found herself calling out his name. Not "Stud" or "Hubby" or any variation of the two, but "Troy," long and loud and at the top of her lungs.

He didn't let her coming inconvenience him in the slightest as he kept thrusting away and staring at her as if she were indeed the most beautiful woman in the world.

It was hard to compose herself and create any semblance of swagger after such an intense orgasm. But her name wouldn't have been Jazz Stewart if she hadn't tried.

"I can handle anything you bring my way, Hubbalino." Her voice was more of a breathless pant than the strong, sexy, confident tone she was aiming for. "Can you handle it?" She tilted her hips and squeezed her thighs around him, pulling him closer and deeper into her.

His eyes narrowed in challenge and his thrusts became even more purposeful. Every nerve ending in her body became ultra-aware and overly stimulated. She pulsed with a desire that threatened to consume her. And she knew that if she went up in flames, she was taking him right along with her. She pursed her lips and narrowed her eyes right back at him as their bodies swayed in a sexual dance-off where the winner would not only take all, they would also give their all.

"I can take anything you're willing to give me, Jasmine. *Anything*."

That admission sent her spiraling over the top once again. Her body began to shake and her thighs quivered and she clenched them around him even tighter.

"You can have anything you want, Troy." She kissed him passionately. "Anything…"

He let out a howling sound that came from deep in his gut and threw his head back when she broke away from the kiss. She felt his body shake and then go completely still.

He kissed her one last time before getting up, swooping her into his arms and heading for the bedroom.

Troy opened his eyes and tried to get his bearings. Jasmine had her head on his chest and he had his arms wrapped around her. He was holding her closer than close. In fact, it was safe to say that he—Mr. Never-Let-Them-Stay-the-Night—was cuddling.

They had made love twice more after their first time in the living room, and he could feel himself reacting to her soft skin and plush curves. His erection sprang to life at the thought of being inside of her again.

She must have felt it because she lifted her head up from his chest and stared at him incredulously. "I need food if I'm going to keep up with your insatiable sex appetite."

He kissed her and let his fingers explore her moist slick folds. "I promise to feed you as soon as we're done." He lifted her leg to his shoulder and entered her warmth.

Either he was tripping or Jasmine had him under some kind of a spell, because the few times he'd been with her increasingly topped one another and each felt like the best sex he'd ever had.

He placed her other leg on his shoulder and rocked slowly in and out of her, letting the friction build and build with each move.

"Maybe it's a good thing for us to get this out of our systems now. The novelty will wear off and then we can get back to the way things were." She panted out her words and she lifted her hips to meet his thrusts.

Before he'd actually made love to her, he might have been foolish enough to believe that. He had even thought that sex between them might help take off the edge of him wanting her so much since kissing her on their wedding day. But if anything, having her only made him want her more and want more from her than she was probably ready to give.

Like the fact that even though they were technically married and would have probably been trying to have a family and not using condoms because of that, he hadn't used any protection yet. And he didn't want to. He was having these weird desires to see her belly rounded with his seed.

He bent and took her delicious nipple into his mouth. The beautiful, plump, toasted-cinnamon breast with the dark-toffee areola and milk-chocolate nipple tasted sweeter than any candy concoction ever could.

"Ahhh!" She threw her head back and wrapped her arms around his shoulders, holding his head in place as he suckled and she rode out her orgasm.

He could feel her sex tightening around his, milking him with ferocious want and need. He clenched his teeth, determined to endure the tantalizing massage that tempted him to the edge of his own explosion.

But it felt too good and he was only human. He found himself screaming out her name as soon as her shaking body went limp with satisfaction. He shook with his own release seconds later. He moved her legs and rolled over on his back carrying her with him and keeping the connection.

She rested on top of him for several minutes. The

only sound in the room was their heavy, satiated breathing. He let his hands slide down her back and cup her voluptuous behind.

She lifted her head and glared at him. "Food. Feed me, Seymour." Her head fell back to his chest.

He sighed and gently rolled her onto the bed. If he was going to get any more of what he was starting to think he couldn't live without, he needed to feed his wife.

My wife. Mine…

He was starting to like the sound of that.

Chapter 6

You've been played!

Monday morning came too soon. After a weekend of helping Jasmine get settled into his place and getting to know every inch of his wife's body in the most intimate of ways, it was time to go back to work.

He had to admit that he was enjoying getting to know little things about her as a person. He learned that even though she went on and on about cooking being overrated, she was actually a really good cook and could make all the Bajan delicacies he'd come to love when he visited there. She made excellent macaroni pie, stew chicken, rice and peas and a very tasty shepherd's pie.

She made him swear not to tell anyone she cooked for him if he ever wanted it to happen again. And since he rather liked her cooking, he was inclined to keep quiet.

And he also learned that she used serial dating as a shield to protect herself because her mother had drilled into her head that men were no good. She didn't tell him that, and she probably never would. But he picked it up from the seemingly random things she had shared with him about Carlyne.

He also learned that he was determined to prove to her that she didn't have to protect her heart around him. That he wanted to protect her heart, and she could trust him to keep it safe. Needless to say, that realization shocked him. He wasn't sure how he felt about it and he certainly wasn't ready to share it with her just yet.

"These pancakes are good, Hubby." She wiped her mouth with a napkin and winked at him. She looked hot in a vibrant purple sweater dress that hugged her curves the way he wanted to and the sexiest thigh-high leather boots he'd ever seen. She seemed poised and ready to take Detroit by storm.

"Thanks, Jasmine."

She pursed her lips and took a sip of her coffee.

"Before we head off to work, I think I really should tell you about my new job—" she started.

"No. Don't tell me." The last thing he wanted to do was break her trust. And if it was hot news that he could share with his viewers on *Detroit Live,* he couldn't promise he wouldn't share it.

He liked to think that he wouldn't do that, but it was better not to tempt things. "I told you I can't promise I won't spill the beans. And you don't need to risk getting sued by your new boss or getting fired. Although, I suppose we could find a spot for you at Singleton Communication…"

She nibbled on her lips in contemplation and he wanted to reach across the table and kiss her. His mind started to envision all the things he could do with the Mrs. Butterworth syrup and her splayed across the table.

Pancakes be damned!

He could have a hungry man's breakfast of Jasmine's sweet toasted-cinnamon skin covered in maple syrup.

He licked his lips. He'd have to table the table action for later or they would never make it to work.

"Don't worry, after your new boss makes the announcement, all of Detroit will know. And if you're the new competition, I'll try and go easy on you. But you should know, this is my city. *Detroit*

Live is the show to beat for one reason and one reason only… I'm all that!"

"Wow!" She narrowed her eyes and shook her head. "There's that humongous ego of yours. I was wondering where it went these past weeks."

He shrugged.

He really wasn't conceited, not when it came to his work anyway.

No. When it came to him hosting *Detroit Live* and him being the face of entertainment news in the city, well, he was just convinced. He was the best. And there was nothing anyone, not even his father, the man who signed his checks, could do about it. Hopefully, when he went in today—after being away and not doing live shows for two weeks—his father would have seen reason and would stop harassing him about moving from in front of the camera and joining the suits in the Singleton Communication offices.

He shook his head.

Enough of that!

Looking at his beautiful wife wearing the evil frown he had begun to miss since they had gotten married and had started to become closer, he couldn't help but smile. "You should be smiling, Jasmine. It's not like I'm lying. I am all that, and you get to be married to me. You're a lucky girl. Do you know how many women all around the world are going to be heartbroken once the news of our marriage really gets out there?"

She sucked her teeth long and lyrically. "C'dear, I ain' got time for dis foolishness dis mornin', yuh hear? I ain' know why I does let yuh work muh nerves, nuh. But I agree with yuh on one ting. Yuh can wait and hear wit de rest of de city who gwa run dis town. She name Jazz Stewart! Mark my words!" She sucked her teeth again and got up.

He could only laugh as he watched the seductive sway of her hips as she walked away from him.

Life with Jasmine was anything but boring.

After breakfast, Troy took his time getting to work. The show didn't tape until two. If he showed up too early, it would just give his father more time to nag him about settling down, being responsible and joining the business end of the company. Troy actually couldn't wait to see the look on his father's face once he told him that he was married and he still wasn't going to stop hosting *Detroit Live* and become an old businessman. The thought of one-upping his father made him a little more excited about getting to work and having the same old battle again.

Once he reached the Singleton Communication studios where the live audience segments of *Detroit Live* were taped, he noticed that just about everyone was gathered in Studio B.

Studio B was always set for *Detroit Live*. So Troy really couldn't fathom why everyone on staff and media folk from all the local networks would be gathered there without him. A sense of foreboding crept through his chest, and it went deeper into his gut when he heard his father's voice.

"I'd like to thank you all for coming here today. This is a very exciting time for Singleton Communication and *Detroit Live*." Jordan Singleton's deep voice boomed so loudly he hardly needed the microphone.

Troy's father was an older, more distinguished version of Troy. Jordan Singleton stood over six feet tall like his son. They shared the same caramel complexion and the same broad smile and dimpled chin. Where Troy's hair was black deep-set waves, Jordan's wave sported a more-salt-than-pepper mixture. Both men were built tough but wore a suave swagger that belied the toughness that went right down to their cores.

Troy made his way through to the front of the crowded room wondering what the hell was going on and knowing that he wouldn't like it when he found out.

Once he could see what had everyone's attention, his stomach dropped. His father was standing on the *Detroit Live* stage and Jasmine was standing next to him.

Jasmine noticed him the same time that he noticed her, and their eyes held for what felt like forever. He squinted in question, willing her to tell him what this was all about. She broke eye contact with him then and kept her eyes on his father.

"I'd like to introduce you to the new cohost of *Detroit Live,* Jazz Stewart. Jazz will be cohosting the show, and my son, Troy Singleton, will remain on as the other cohost. Jazz comes to us from Boston, where she was an up-and-coming media darling and girl about town. She brings a smart, sexy, witty and very feminine side to what has been a somewhat masculine take on the entertainment happenings of our fair city." Jordan primped and preened for all the cameras like he'd been born to do so. The man had always been a ham.

Troy figured that was where he'd gotten his own love of the spotlight and desire to always be the center of attention from.

The room started buzzing, and Troy could feel the tension of all the people wondering how he was taking the news.

"And since she brings a fresh perspective, we decided to up the ante a little bit. *Detroit Live* will be having its very own battle of the sexes. You all will get to weigh in on which host you like best, and that host will be the only host of the show at the end of six months. It's all up to you. Will you root for Team Jazz or Team Troy?"

The room really started buzzing then, and before Troy knew it he was walking up to the stage. Jasmine still wouldn't look at him. She kept her focus on his dad, and that just made Troy angrier.

Although fuming, Troy had to give it to his wife. She was quite the little actress. When he jumped up onstage, she feigned shock like a pro.

He couldn't help it. Unable to stop himself, he had to see how good she really was. So he walked over to her, pulled her into his arms and kissed her.

She kissed him back with so much passion they were both panting by the time his father cleared his throat for them to stop.

Troy smirked at his father. "Dad, since this seems to be the day for big announcements, I should let you know that Jasmine is my wife. You can call her Jasmine Stewart-Singleton now."

Jasmine bristled and she leveled him with a harsh stare.

She didn't miss a beat as she let him know, "Yeah…about that…my work name will always be *Jazz Stewart*. Since that's my 'brand' and it has more pop. But don't worry, Hubby, at home, I'll always be *Mrs. Singleton*."

She smiled and gave him another light peck on

the lips so that only he was able to catch the glare in her eyes.

Angrily, he glared right back at her.

Troy turned to his father, who was eying them both suspiciously. "I have to hand it to you, Dad. You picked the one woman in the world that I might think twice about wiping the floor with. But I'm sorry, wifey, you're going down."

"We'll see about that, Hubby. I think you'll soon realize the truth. And the truth is, I'm taking you out!"

The crowd went wild and cameras flashed as they both stood glaring at each other. Jazz with her arms akimbo and him with his arms folded across his chest.

Neither of them managed to best Jordan, who seemed to sense a media gold mine and proclaimed, "Their marriage makes this competition even more interesting…" Jordan Singleton hammed it up for the camera and added, "Who will win, the husband or the wife? Only the ratings will tell. Tune in, Detroit. Or not…" He gestured toward the married couple. "The choice is up to you."

He's going to divorce me. I just know it. He's going to divorce me and then my deadbeat father is going to get all of my mother's hard-earned money. And then I'm going to be left alone and I'll never feel those magnificent hands doing all kinds of scandalous things to my body ever again…

Jazz was the picture of calm on the outside as she and Troy followed Jordan Singleton back to his office. She held her shoulders straight and kept pace with the long-legged men as if she, too, towered over six feet instead of her average height of five-six.

But on the inside every horrible thing that could possibly happen now that Troy knew the truth ran through her head. And if anyone would have told her that she would care more about the fact that she might lose the husband she never even knew she wanted than she would if she lost the job she'd always dreamed of, she would have called him or her a crazy liar.

But it was what it was. The only thing she cared about at that moment was how she was going to make Troy understand and forgive her.

Once they were in Jordan's office, he eyed them both suspiciously.

She put on her best game face and wondered why she was standing there wishing Troy would hold her hand or something. Just because he had been her rock for the past few weeks as she dealt with the loss of her mother didn't mean she could count on him every time she was feeling unsure or under fire.

"Before I get started and find out just what the

hell is going on between the two of you, Jazz, let me say that I'm sorry to hear about your mother. Carlyne was a wonderful woman and she will be missed. Now, what's this about the two of you being married?"

When Jordan mentioned her mother she went absolutely still. She knew that the two of them had met a few times when Carlyne had come with her to attend various functions for Alicia, Darren and their children, but she hadn't been expecting him to mention her mother.

Troy must have sensed her becoming upset, because he reached over, squeezed her hand and held it.

"That said," Jordan resumed, "what I'd like to know now is how did the two of you all of a sudden end up married? And does it have anything to do with the fact that I pegged Jazz here for your replacement when you take your proper place in the company? Did she tell you that she had been hired to cohost *Detroit Live?* Jazz, did you break your confidentiality clause? I really hope you didn't. Just because you're apparently family now doesn't mean I won't sue you."

Jazz straightened at the threat of a lawsuit. "Now, how was I supposed to tell him anything, when I didn't know the details? I thought I was just going to be the new cohost. And I figured he would be irritated about that since it was his show and his alone and no one likes sharing something that they used to have all to themselves. Trust me when I tell you that was the last thing I wanted to tell my new husband. But I had no idea you planned to have us in some kind of a competition! No, Jordan, I didn't break the confidentiality clause."

But I really wish I had…

She chanced a glance at Troy, but he was staring straight ahead. Even though he held her hand in his, she felt strangely disconnected from him. The odd thing was she didn't know when she'd become so connected to him in the first place. She only knew that she wanted that closeness back.

Jordan Singleton eyed Troy and Jazz with a mixture of suspicion and trepidation. "Well, I really hope you're telling the truth, Jazz, and I don't find out otherwise. Because I will fire you and sue you if I find out otherwise…family or not! Speaking of which, how did you come to be married to my son?"

"I ran into Jasmine when I was coming back from the Barbados Jazz festival. She had just buried her mother and was looking rather distraught," Troy started.

Jazz struggled not to roll her eyes when she remembered how Troy had told her she looked like death warmed over. She painted on a bright smile.

"Even though it had to be the worst time of my life, seeing Troy was a bright spot in an otherwise gloomy situation. I've always thought he was a hot stud, you know." She turned to Troy and grinned.

She tried not to crack up at the clenched-teeth smile he offered her in return. "Well, I've always had a fondness for Jasmine, no matter how harsh and mouthy she tended to be most times. I couldn't just let her travel alone in her condition. I knew she was moving to Detroit soon. Even though I didn't know she was moving here to help you stab me in the back." He let go of her hand and she felt a stabbing pain in her heart. "So I went with her to Boston and something special happened between us. Before I knew it, we were on the plane to Vegas eloping."

"Mmm-hmm… Well, I suppose the two of you have known each other for years. So, it's not like you just met her yesterday and married her today. I guess you two know what you're doing. And if not, the entire state of Michigan might be watching it all implode on air. The ratings would be amazing, like those God-awful reality TV shows."

Troy smirked. "It'll be ratings magic. And now that I think about it, Dad, I can't help but wonder if you hired Jasmine on purpose. Maybe you sensed how I felt about her all along and knew she was the one woman I might think twice about beating out of a job. And then you'd have what you wanted—me off of *Detroit Live* and in a stuffy office."

Jordan didn't say anything and the two men just sized each other up. Jazz thought Troy's comment added a nice umph to their case. Of course he hadn't really felt anything but dislike for her in the past, but his comment nicely threw the ball of blame into Jordan's court.

"But, Dad, you and my adorable new wife should know one thing… *Detroit Live* is my baby and anyone getting in the way of that is going to be ruined." He turned to Jazz. "Even you, sweetheart."

She smiled at him with every ounce of syrupy sweetness she could muster. "We'll see just who gets ruined, Hubby Bubby."

"Yes, we will indeed." Jordan tented his hands under his chin as he looked back and forth between Jazz and Troy. "This has the potential to be phenomenal in the ratings. Man against wife… The promotional team is going to have a field day with this one! This could be even better than my original plans for the competition." He smiled at them as if they had both turned into golden geese. "Why don't the two of you go and enjoy one more day of honeymoon before we kick things off? I'll have the folks in promotion and marketing come up with new concepts playing this husband-and-wife thing. The other promo for the contest was bland compared to this. This is the Battle of the Sexes kicked up a notch. We can show another rerun today, since we've been showing them the past two weeks." He peered at Troy. "Word of advice, son, *no one* is irreplaceable, not even you. The next time you decide to teach me a lesson by taking off, jet-setting and eloping and whatnot, remember that piece of information."

Troy didn't respond, but Jazz could tell he was beyond angry. She could feel the seething rolling off of him in waves.

"Jordan, you can't really expect me and him to compete against one another for the show. He's my husband—"

"So? This is a business. I didn't tell you two to get married." Jordan laughed and rubbed his palms together. "I'm glad you did, because this contest could be a real cash cow."

"But I don't want to be pitted against him—"

"Would you rather be sued?"

"Okay, Dad. Stop threatening my wife with lawsuits! We'll do your little contests. But in the end, when I win my show, you'd better come up with another show for Jasmine."

"Come up with another show for me? You mean he better come up with another show for you after I win."

How dare he just assume I'm going to lose!

Troy smirked at her and stood up to leave. "Yeah, whatever. Picture that? I'm out of here."

Jazz stared after her husband for a minute before turning back to her new father-in-law.

Jordan eyed her with concern. "Are you really doing okay with your mom's passing?"

She swallowed and nodded. She didn't know if she would continue to be okay if Troy divorced her. But thanks to his strength and being able to lean on him, she was doing a heck of a lot better than she had been.

"I'm glad my son was there for you in your time of need. And I'm glad you two fell in love and got married. The two of you are in love, aren't you?"

Jazz's eyes widened as the realization hit her, almost knocking her out of her seat. She had been so focused on mourning her mother, worrying about the stupid will and getting used to being married to her former nemesis that she hadn't even realized it was happening...

A warm, tingling sensation started in her heart and then coursed through her body finally landing in her brain.

She was in love with Troy Singleton.

And she was in trouble because there was no way he could possibly love her.

He was probably going to divorce her, and it didn't even matter that her deadbeat father would be getting the money. The money didn't even matter. The only thing that mattered was she loved Troy Singleton and he probably hated her more now than he ever did when they were frenemies.

"Do you love my son, Jazz?" Jordan asked.

Jazz nodded. "Yes, I do."

"Well, then, everything will work out fine. This contest won't hurt your marriage if the two of you really love one another. And trust me, if my eternally single, bachelor-for-life-son married you, he must be in love. Love is the only thing that could make that boy give up his player card."

She swallowed.

Jordan didn't know the half of it. Helping out a friend and the possibility of being able to stick it to his father were two other reasons Troy would get married.

She fiddled her hands in her lap and nibbled on her bottom lip. "Well, I'm going to meet some of the staff for the show and then head back home. I'll see you tomorrow."

"Okay, Jazz. And don't worry. Things will be fine. Everything has a way of working out the way it's supposed to, no matter what we do. Things between you and Troy will end up the way they are supposed to. I have faith in that. And I think your mother would've had faith in that as well."

She just stared at him for a moment, wondering

why he kept bringing up her mother. It was almost as if he knew something. But she had no idea what he could possibly know. It wasn't as if he and her mother had been close friends or anything like that. He couldn't possibly know about the money and the will. And she certainly wasn't about to bring it up, or ask him. Then he'd know the real reason behind her sham of a marriage to Troy.

So she just nodded and hightailed it out of there.

The only thing she could think about was how she was going to be able to fall out of love with Troy Singleton.

Troy sat in his home office going over and over the day's events, which caused him to go over and over the events of the past week, all in an effort to figure out how exactly it came to be that the player had been played.

The smallest bedroom in his home had been custom-designed with cabinetry, a desk and shelves all built to fit the space at the maximum level of efficiency. Even though the room had been designed with work in mind, it still met the level of style he and his decorator, a lovely woman whose name he could never remember, had achieved with the rest of the house. From the mocha Caesar Stone countertops to the espresso wood Shaker-style door and shelves, the room had the same depth and strength as the rest of his home.

"So are you just going to give me the silent treatment forever or do you plan on acting like a grown-up soon?"

He looked up to find Jasmine standing in front of him with her hands on her hips. She had the nerve to look upset, when he was the one who had been betrayed by his father and her.

Confidentiality clause his ass!

She knew he would have had a problem with having a cohost! She should have told him that before he married her. But then he probably wouldn't have married her. And then he wouldn't have known how sweet she tasted and how good it felt to go to sleep holding her in his arms. And he never would have been made to own and admit how much he really secretly liked their verbal sparring matches and adored the way her flashes of Bajan heat brought such joy to his heart and made him smile.

He glanced up at her. She had changed into a pair of jeans and a sweater from the sexy purple sweater dress and thigh-high boots she'd worn earlier. The jeans hugged her curves like a glove and the red sweater clung to her perfect breasts in a way that made him want to reach out and touch.

He shook it off.

"Jasmine, I really don't think you want me talking

to you right now. Trust me, you want me to cool off some." He dismissively waved her away after breaking eye contact.

"Why drag out the inevitable? You hate me and you want a divorce, right?"

"I don't hate you, Jasmine."

"But you want a divorce, right?"

He sighed. Here was his escape hatch. He'd married her, made unbelievably mind-blowing love to her and for all intents and purposes, the old Troy would have been through with her and would have happily divorced her and moved on to the next one.

But this was Jasmine. His Jasmine. His wife for as long as she would have him, no matter what kind of contest his father had cooked up. He didn't want it to end yet.

Even more so, he really didn't want to question or examine why he didn't want it to end.

He just wasn't ready. He wasn't ready to let her go and he wasn't ready to question why.

He heard a soft, whistle-like sigh come out of Jasmine's mouth, and her shoulders sort of slouched. "You do want a divorce." This time it was a statement instead of a question. She turned to leave.

"I don't want a divorce, Jasmine. I just need a minute to process everything. I don't think we should have this conversation when I'm so—"

"Angry?"

He nodded.

"I don't want you to be angry with me. I swear I didn't know that your father planned to make us compete for the hosting position. I did know that I was going to be your cohost and that you would be a little upset about it. But I thought we could work through that because we'd make a good team. I really think we'd be great as cohosts. There's a...I don't know...there's something there when we do our little back-and-forth verbal scrimmages... I thought it could be kind of hot, you know. I never wanted to be in a competition with you. I just wanted to work with you."

She sighed again, and the sound pierced his heart.

He stood up and wrapped his arms around her. Although he was still upset, he didn't like seeing her upset. Apparently his little wife had him wrapped around her finger, and it had happened without either of them even realizing it.

"Chemistry." He whispered in her ear just before he nipped it.

She gulped as she melted in his arms.

"Chemistry is the word you're looking for to describe what we have, Jasmine. It's what we've had from the first minute we met. It was too much for either of us at the time, and it became combustible.

But it has simmered over the years, and for better or worse, we are married now. And I'm not letting you go just yet." He released her and gave her a playful smack on her ample behind.

"Besides, since you're my competition now, I have to be sure to keep an eye on you. It'll work to my benefit keeping you around." He sat back down at his desk.

He could see the fire burning in his lovely wife and it turned him on considerably.

She smiled a smile that was equally sexy and sinister. "Keep your friends close and your frenemies closer?"

He grinned. It was actually more like keep the woman you were starting to become irrevocably attached to as close as you possibly could and never-ever let her go. But she didn't need to know that yet.

So he shrugged and smirked his best cocky smirk. "Something like that."

Her eyes narrowed and she gave him an appraising look before turning and walking away. He thought about following her as he watched her hips sway, but then thought better of it. He was still trying to figure things out. And until he did, maybe it was best to slow things down a bit with Jasmine…

Chapter 7

Game recognize game

"So, Detroit, this is your boy Troy signing off—" Troy started his signature goodbye words at the end of the show.

Jazz cut him off. She added herself to the mix and finished his closing. "And this is your girl Jazz… And *we* want you to remember to keep it fresh, keep it funky and keep it all the way live! See you tomorrow, Detroit! Stay peace."

She had watched enough of his tapes to know that's how he closed the show each and every time, and she thought it was okay. She would have gone for something a little catchier. But she figured it would be a nod of collaboration if she didn't come in with her own closing too soon. She envisioned changing it eventually to suit her own tastes. His closing sounded a little too *Soul Train* for her. But she knew it was best to invoke her changes slowly.

As soon as the cameras went off, Troy turned to her and glared. "Can I speak with you for a moment, Jasmine? In the back, please?" His voice was clipped and he seemed a little irritated.

She had no idea what he could have been so irritated about. It was only their first show, but she was feeling really good about it. Everything had gone well. The live audience seemed to love the banter between her and Troy and they laughed when they were supposed to. The audience watching at home probably loved it, too.

Once they entered his dressing room she folded her arms across her chest. "What's the problem, Hubby? I think the show went great."

"The problem is you ate my line."

She pursed her lips. "Umm, no…we shared the closing. Just like we now share the show." She arched her eyebrow slightly as she watched him huff and bristle. "Like it or not, Troy, we are cohosts until one of us is the only host. So we might as well suck it up and put on the best show we can."

"It's my closing line, *Jasmine*."

"I know that, *Hubby*. That's why I didn't change it and said the line the way you *always* say it *every single* closing, even though I—" She cut herself off. It probably wouldn't do any good to insult the man when he was all huffy and mad.

He narrowed his eyes and clenched his teeth. "Even though what?"

She shrugged. "It's no biggie. Forget I even said anything."

"Even though what, Jasmine?"

"Even though Don Cornelius called and said he'd like his line back. Love, Peace and *So-ul!*" She tried to call back her laughter, but it came bubbling forth.

Troy picked up a pillow from the small sofa and tossed it at her. "I see somebody has jokes. I suppose you think you could come up with a better closing?"

She caught the pillow and threw it back at him before mumbling, "Sure couldn't do worse."

"I heard that, smart mouth."

She laughed and turned to leave but not before mumbling a parting shot. "Good, do something about it then."

When she reached the door and opened it she wasn't surprised that Troy had walked up behind her and closed it. She could feel his tall muscular frame behind her as the door shut.

She turned around and eyed him with interest.

He hadn't come to bed last night until late and he had gotten up earlier than she had. They hadn't really talked since he'd told her that he wasn't ready to talk. She was surprised they had been able to do their first show today.

She nibbled on her lower lip and tilted her head. "Have you decided that you want to talk to me? I mean really talk to me now?"

"I could think of a lot of things I want to do to you, Jasmine, and talking isn't anywhere on the list."

She frowned. "Well, if you can't talk to me and you're going to hold a grudge, then you can't have sex with me, either."

Where the hell did that come from? Hold on now, girly. Don't be so rash...

Even though her body seemed to be railing against her words, in her mind she knew she was right. If Troy was so upset with her that he couldn't talk to her and they couldn't hash out their issues, then sex would only muddy things up even more.

But damn....

He pressed closer and she could feel his desire to do anything but talk to her pressing against her stomach. The feel of him and the memory of him made her think that not talking might not be such a bad idea.

She shook her head. "I mean it, Hubinator. Don't try and tempt me with your big ole sexy body and your big ole—well…I won't be tempted. So you can just back up off me and try and take it down a notch."

He bent over and brushed his lips across her forehead. "She thinks I'm sexy." He moved further down and pressed his lips against hers. "She thinks I'm tempting."

"I think you're a jerk and you're not playing fair. Don't forget, Hubilina, two can play that game."

"Hubilina? Okay, I really don't care for that one. Hubby was bad enough."

"When you start calling me Jazz, which by the way you *have* to do on the show. If you noticed, I called you Troy during the taping because that's your professional name. I'd appreciate it if you called me Jazz when we are on air and tapping the show."

He moved away then and walked back over to his chair. "Yeah, that's not gonna happen."

She sighed as she decided which battle she was going to fight today. Like it or not, they had to work together. And like it or not they were married and had to live together. The more important thing was probably getting their relationship, for lack of a better word, on track.

It was clear that Troy didn't really trust her. He'd grown weary of her in just one day. Even though he'd said he didn't want a divorce, that didn't really tell her where she stood.

"Troy?"

His head shot up in shock. "What, no nickname? What happen to Hubby?"

She walked over and placed her hand under his chin so that his head was tilted up toward her. If he stood she'd have to look up at him. She was so used to doing so that she found this new position a little unsettling.

"All my nicknames for you haven't gotten you to call me by my preferred name. So, I'll leave that battle for now. We have more pressing concerns than what we call each other, Troy."

He eyed her suspiciously. "Yeah, right, you're probably thinking of some new irritating nickname for me as we speak."

She shook her head. "I'm not, Troy."

He frowned. "Stop that."

"Stop what? That's your name. *Troy.* See, I can be a big enough person to admit defeat. Nothing I do is going to get you to call me Jazz, so—"

He stood up and she tilted her head to stare at him. "Silly woman. I call you Jazz all the time. Jazz. Mine. Jasmine. It's been my own personal joke for years."

She gulped. "Years." Then she narrowed her eyes in disbelief and repeated, "Years?"

He nodded. "Years, Jasmine."

She sighed. "What's going on between us, Troy?"

"I'm not sure. But I want to find out." He ran his hand across his face in resignation. "I think I'm finally ready to find out."

"Are you still angry with me?" Her heart raced inside her chest as she waited for the answer.

He pulled her onto his lap so that she now straddled him. And he kissed her, long and deep. His tongue marked and claimed territory in her mouth only to be followed by his lips and teeth. She moaned from deep in her gut and reached up to wrap her arms around his neck. Her lips pressed and puckered as he pulled them into his desire.

His arms moved from her waist to her behind and he cupped each buttock in his big, strong hands. He squeezed and caressed as he nibbled and suckled. She moved her hands to his shirt and placed them underneath so that she could feel his heated, muscular frame.

She groaned as she pulled away. She couldn't go there with him if he was still angry with her. "I'm sorry, Troy. I truly am. I should have told you your father's company hired me and I'd be your cohost. I should have told you before marrying you and definitely before we—"

"Made love?" Troy finished her sentence.

She nodded. "I'm sorry."

"I forgive you. And I'm not angry with you."

"So are we going to set some new ground rules now that you know about my job, and now that we're competing for the same slot? I can move into the guest room… I mean… I totally understand if you want to put some distance between us now." She braced herself for the answer she knew had to be coming.

"I definitely don't want that." Holding her, with her straddling his hips, he stood up from the chair they'd been in and walked her over to the sofa in his dressing room. Sitting, he pulled her closer to him so that she fit more snugly on his lap.

"I'm pretty sure there's no turning back, Jasmine. We've been avoiding this for years, but now that we've started down this road, there's no turning back."

She rested her head on his chest and listened to his firm and steady heartbeat. There were a million things she could have said. Instead she just inhaled and exhaled deeply, taking in his scent and the comfort of his embrace.

"Alicia and Sonya want to take me out this week for the bachelorette party they say you cheated me out of by eloping. They said you guys can watch the kids while we go out on the town."

He chuckled. "Tell them not to take my wife to

some cheesy strip joint with overly buff Chippendale dancers."

"I most certainly will." She feigned indignation. "A cheesy strip joint for *moi*? I don't think so. Only the *cheesiest* of strip joints will do. And I've never had a fondness for Chippendale dancers, not enough diversity. Give me a buff Little Ray-Ray or Tyrone from the block any day."

He laughed and she looked up at him as she joined in.

"We're going to be okay?" A year ago, no one could have told her she would have even asked that question in regard to herself and Troy. Hell, a month ago she thought she could have cared less about the self-proclaimed playboy. But now everything she held dear depended on the answer to that question.

"Yes, I believe we will."

"Okay, now tell me this story again," Sonya slurred after her second margarita.

They had decided to come to the happy hour at an authentic Mexican bar and grill in Greektown. The nachos and bargain-priced drinks seemed like a great idea at the time…

Jazz sighed. It was only the seventh or eighth time she had told the story of how she and Troy saw each other in the airport and fell in love soon after. She had told the story so much she was starting to believe it herself.

After a week of working and living with her former arch-nemesis who had somehow turned into the, unbeknownst to him, love of her life, she needed this girls' night out.

She and Troy had worked out a seamless work routine. They had a rapport and camaraderie in front of the camera that very few could rival. And if she didn't personally have her eye on Oprah's pie and eventually hosting her own talk show, she might have been inclined to tell Regis and Kelly they ought to watch their backs. She and Troy were just that good.

"I do not want to hear that bogus-ass story yet again. Jazz, I know you don't think we believe that. Y'all might have had me a little fooled in the hospital last week. But that was because I had just given birth and the labor had me out of it. Now that I've had time to mull over this so-called marriage, I realize there is a lot you aren't telling us." Alicia took another sip from her virgin strawberry daiquiri.

Jazz rolled her eyes at her two sorority sisters and friends. She and the beautiful but very opinionated Alicia went all the way back to freshman year at college. When they had first met, she didn't think that she and the absolutely stunning Black American Princess would hit it off. Alicia, with her hazel eyes, milk-chocolate skin and long, curly, jet-black hair, had a long-legged strut that would have made runway models jealous. Jazz was more of an earthy beauty, with brown eyes, thicker hair, thicker lips and definitely a thicker body.

When Sir Mix-a-Lot rapped, "Red beans and rice didn't miss her," all he needed to do was add a line about rice and peas and he would have had Jazz covered. She had back and lots of it. And then there was the fact that Alicia came from money, old money, and Jazz didn't. But somehow they became the best of friends in spite of or maybe because of all their differences. And Jazz got a front-row seat into Alicia's world and met Sonya and the other old-money Detroit black blue bloods.

Sonya was a shade or two lighter than her brother, Troy. And she wore her long chemically straightened light-brown hair back with a headband. If Jazz thought she and Alicia didn't have anything in common when they first met, she knew for sure that she and Sonya were probably as diametrically opposed as any two people could ever be. Where being a black debutante had been a rite of passage that went back several generations for Sonya, the only reason Jazz had any kind of similar passage into womanhood was because the Boston Alumnae Chapter of Delta sponsored a Delta Debutante Cotillion and her teacher, who had been a member of the chapter, saw something in Jazz that she wanted to nurture.

Jazz's mother had never had time for those kinds of things, but she encouraged her daughter to take part. That experience was the reason Jazz ended up pledging Delta when she went to college. And this reminded her of yet another way that she was different from her two friends. They were both Delta legacies from several generations of Delta women, and her mother hadn't been able to attend college because she had a child to raise. But none of that mattered now, because these two women were the closest things she had to sisters. And she hated lying to them…

"Okay, here we go… Sonya, no, I will not tell you the story again. I'm tired of it already and you know it's bad when you make a woman tired of hearing her own love story. Sheesh. And, Alicia, that is the full extent of the story and all the story you're going to get. My goodness! Can't a girl have any modesty these days? Do you really want to hear all about how he put it on me until I didn't know if I was coming or going and had me speaking in tongues?"

"Yes!" Alicia and Sonya said in unison.

"Well, too bad, there are some things a lady has to keep between her and her man!" Jazz laughed. They were a hot mess and she loved them.

"Booo, you used to be fun. Now you're turning into a mean old married lady." Alicia sipped her virgin drink and joined Jazz in laughter.

"Yeah, we used to be able to live vicariously through all of your exploits. Now that you've married my brother, you're no fun." Sonya rolled her eyes and then she narrowed them. "And you better not hurt my big brother with all your player mack momma ways. He may be a slut puppy, but he's a nice guy, and if he married you and gave you our grandmother's ring, then he must really love you. So, don't break his heart or I'll forget we're friends and you're my soror and I'll kick your butt."

Seeing Troy's normally proper sister slightly inebriated and threatening violence would have been funny if Jazz wasn't worried about her own heart getting broken.

"Ple-ase, if anything we have to worry about Troy breaking Jazz's heart. That's why I have Darren giving him a good talking to right now. Troy has been sniffing around Jazz for years and she wouldn't give him any play. He probably married her as a last-ditch effort to get in her pants. I'm sorry now that I tried to play matchmaker when I got married and had him pick her up from the airport. I feel awful about that! I put you smack dab in the middle of the player's sights." Alicia reached over and gave her a hug.

Jazz arched her eyebrow and studied her friend in mock concern. "Are you sure they're giving you virgin daiquiris? Because you must be drunk or have lost your mind if you think any man is going to break my heart." Jazz rolled her eyes and gave a steups for good measure. "Yuh mus' be crazy for truth if yuh tink dat."

Jazz speaking in dialect must have triggered a memory of Jazz's mother for Alicia because her friend became almost weepy then. If they weren't giving her alcohol in those daiquiris then it must have been the post-pregnancy hormones that had Alicia so emotional.

"Oh, I miss your mom, Jazz. Carlyne was like a second mother to me." Alicia hugged Jazz. "Oh, and I miss your mom, too, Sonya."

A confused expression crossed Sonya's face. "My mother isn't dead."

"Yeah, but since the divorce and since she started having her midlife crises, she has been globetrotting more than your player brother and she has more boy toys than even Jazz used to have. So I miss the mother she used to be before she lost her damn mind." Alicia busted out laughing.

If Jazz were going to start feeling sorry for herself about her mother's death it went away with Alicia's outrageous statement to Sonya.

"You are a nut, Alicia!" Jazz said as she joined in with Alicia's infectious giggling.

Sonya rolled her eyes. "That is not funny, Alicia. I'm going to tell her when I talk to her."

"Yeah, that's if you remember after one more margarita, girlfriend," Alicia quipped. Then she smirked. "Bartender, get this woman another margarita, please."

Sonya glared at Alicia, but she didn't turn down the drink. Jazz got another piña colada and tried to enjoy the rest of the night out with the girls without wondering exactly what Darren was saying to Troy and if Alicia and Sonya were right to be concerned that Troy might break her heart.

Troy had been home for a good hour and a half by the time Jazz made it home. He'd gotten tired of Darren and Kendrick getting in his business and wanting to know things about his relationship with Jazz that he hadn't exactly figured out himself yet.

All he knew was what started out as a mutual favor between somewhat friends had become something else entirely. And the stakes were higher.

He was in a position to lose a whole lot more than just his television show.

He hadn't made love to her since the day before he found out about her being his cohost on Detroit Live. There were times when he hadn't been able to help kissing her or caressing her, but he had managed, *barely,* to refrain from making love to her again.

It had been a long week, and being around her without having her had made him more than a little irritable. The more he thought about it, Darren and

Kendrick were actually lucky that he hadn't cursed them out.

He was relaxing in his man chair when Jazz came through the door. She carefully hung up her coat and put away her purse before walking over to him. The care and caution she took as she put away her things and walked over were the very reasons he didn't notice that she was slightly tipsy until she got right in front of him.

She looked at him for a full minute and a funny expression came over her face before she plopped down on his lap.

"Whoa. Somebody has had a little too much to drink."

"No I haven't. I'm just feeling a little…ni-ce."

"Hmm… I'd bet money that you bypassed nice about two drinks before your last and you're more in the ki-nd category right about now."

She laughed at his joke without catching an attitude, and that's how he knew she was loaded.

"Did Alicia play designated driver tonight? Because I know if my sister Sonya gets more than one drink in her she isn't any good to drive."

"Yeah, Alicia is breast-feeding our little godbaby, so she will be the designated driver for a while now." She perked up a little and asked, "Did you see our goddaughter today?"

"Yes I did. She's getting bigger already. And

looking more and more like her mother every day."

"Aww… I have to go see her tomorrow." She sighed.

"This is *our* chair, Troy. Coming home and seeing you sitting in our chair made me very horny. You haven't made love to me in over a week. Don't you want me anymore? Or was Alicia right and you married me as an elaborate scheme to get in my pants?"

"She said what? What is with Alicia and her nosy husband? The way they are knee-deep in our business you would think they didn't have three kids to worry about."

"I know, right!" Jasmine became so indignant he knew it had to be the alcohol. "And your sister threatened to kick my ass if I hurt you! Can you believe that?"

"Sonya? No. First of all, my sister wouldn't say the a-word. And second of all, she's so prissy and proper she would never threaten anyone."

"Okay she didn't say *ass,* she said *butt,* but it's the same thing. As if we have to worry about me breaking your heart," she mumbled. "They need to be worrying about you breaking my heart."

He chuckled.

Yes, she was definitely drunk.

There was no way in hell his Jasmine would allow

herself to be that vulnerable and put all her cards on the table like that.

"I'd never break your heart, Jasmine." He kissed her on the forehead.

She looked up at him with the most earnest expression in her big brown eyes. "You promise?"

He smiled. "I promise."

She smiled as she fought back a yawn. She placed her head back on his chest. "Good, because I don't need a sister to kick your ass if you do. I'll kick it myself." She stifled another yawn and the next thing he knew a light and lyric snoring sound wafted through the air.

He shook his head. Leave it to Jasmine to threaten him and then fall right to sleep in his arms.

He stood and carried her to the bedroom. Their little discussion had given him a lot to think about.

The next morning he saw that they had been hit by quite a bit of snow. It had accumulated to several inches overnight. He figured that Jasmine would be nursing a slight hangover, so he started the coffee before he woke her up.

She'd said the night before that she wanted to go see their goddaughter, so he figured they could get an early start and maybe catch a movie after. He saw that the guy he paid to plow his driveway had come through. But he still had to handle the sidewalk and path to the front door.

Once the coffee was done, he brought a cup into the bedroom and placed it on the nightstand by Jasmine. She didn't move an inch and hardly seemed to notice the coffee was in the room.

"Jasmine," he started. "Wake up, sweetheart. It's time to start the day. I made coffee."

She made a grumbling, mumbling sound and placed the pillow over her head.

"Jasmine? I know you hear me. Wake up. You said you wanted to go see Ashley today. Time to rise and shine."

She grunted and groaned and pulled the pillow tighter over her head.

"Okay. I'm going out to snow-blow the sidewalk and walkway. Be ready by the time I'm done so we can go see Ashley and the boys. And since we can't very well go visit Alicia and Darren's bunch without going to see Sonya and Kendrick's bunch, we should plan to visit there as well."

He got up. "And if you let your coffee get cold, there's more in the kitchen. You'll just have to get up and get it."

He could have sworn he heard her mumble and mimic the exact words he had just said to her.

After about an hour and a half of snow-blowing, he finally made his way back up the sidewalk.

Jasmine hadn't come out yet, and that meant they were probably going to get a late start.

Then again, maybe they could stay in after all. There was nothing like an afternoon of snowy-day lovemaking to warm the blood.

He smiled as he remembered the last time he and Jasmine had made love. It had only been a week ago, and that was too long. When a man had a wife as vibrant and as sexy as Jasmine, making love to her less than seven times a week was a crime. He should have been making love to her every single day of the week, several times a day. He'd have to rectify that.

Just as he started to think about ways that he could wake her up when he got back inside, a snowball hit him in the chest. He looked up and couldn't tell where it had come from, only to have another snowball get him smack-dab on the side of his head.

This time he saw his little snowball-throwing wife dart around the side of the house.

"Nice arm, Jasmine," he yelled. "But you really don't want to let that hand of yours write a check your behind can't cash." He picked up some snow and started shaping his snowball as he went off after her. Before he made it to the side of the house another snowball hit him in the back and he knew that she had come back around the other side.

It took him a minute to figure out her routine, but he caught her just as she came back around and grabbed her. He fell backward into the snow with her on top of him and then he rolled her over. He held her arms and straddled her.

She struggled to get free. "Let me go."

"Say please."

"Please." She said with about as much sincerity as a used car salesman.

"No." He kissed her instead, and soon they were making out and leaving their impressions of love in the snow.

When he finally stopped kissing her, he noticed that her teeth were chattering. He got up and lifted her out of the snow.

"Go get warmed up. I'm going to put away the snow blower. But when I get inside, I'm coming for you."

She picked up a handful of snow and doused him with it before he could move.

"Promises, promises," she sang out as she made her way back into the house.

Jazz didn't know what came over her when she went outside. She had only meant to go out there and let Troy know that she was ready to leave for Alicia's whenever he was. But something happened to her when she saw him and suddenly she felt like playing. She had to admit that she hadn't had that much fun in the snow since she was a kid and they'd had huge snowball fights when the schools were closed because of snow days.

And she certainly had never made out in the snow so passionately. No wonder it had taken her a minute to realize that she was freezing her butt off! Troy's heated kisses were burning her up from the inside out.

Just as she had gotten out of the last of her snow-damp clothing, she heard the bedroom door open and close. She looked up and saw that Troy had walked in with his hands behind his back.

He had a devilish grin on his face and she knew that meant payback.

"Now, Troy. You wouldn't do anything to an unarmed woman would you?" She took careful steps backward, trying to make her way to the master bathroom so that she could lock herself in while whatever snow weapon he was carrying melted.

"Funny. You had no problem throwing multiple snowballs at an unarmed man."

"True, very true. But I'm a horrible, *horrible* person. And you should aim to do better. Be the bigger man and all that stuff."

He laughed and shook his head. "I'm afraid I can't do that, Jasmine. Now are you going to take your punishment like a woman or are you going to punk up like a little girl?"

She sighed. Her honor was at stake. "I won't go out like a punk. I'll take my punishment... Like a woman..." She fell back onto the bed in a splayed position with her neck bared and everything. She was totally over the top and hamming it up for all it was worth.

"That's a good girl." He walked over to the bed and she saw that he hadn't had snow behind his back. He had an ice bucket. He placed it on the nightstand and started to undress.

His body never ceased to amaze her. He epitomized masculinity in her mind. The tall, solid, muscular strength of him left her in awe. Every ripple and ridge of his frame made her want to run her finger over his skin. His caramel complexion made her want to lick.

But more than anything, she wondered what he planned to do with that ice.

She didn't have to wait long to find out. He finished undressing quickly, grabbed a piece of ice and joined her on the bed. He straddled her, taking the ice and tracing her left nipple with deep concentration.

Her nipple started to tighten almost immediately until it became almost painfully erect. That's when his mouth began to circle the nipple, warming it as he suckled and sending waves of pleasure from her breast to her sex. She moaned in pleasure and didn't even notice that he had grabbed another piece of ice and had started working her other nipple until she felt the same chilly tightening she'd felt previously. Once he was satisfied that she had endured enough, he began to suck and nibble the other nipple until she was again squirming and purring.

The ice that touched her sex almost made her jump out of the bed.

"Shhhh." He kissed her inner thigh as he circled the ice cube around her clit and across her slick folds.

Her eyes rolled to the back of her head and her teeth clenched when he followed the ice with his warm, ever-so-pleasing mouth. The orgasm that ripped through her felt like it had taken a piece of her soul with it. She felt like she was drifting to the ceiling.

All it took was his first thrust into her to bring her crashing back down.

He began his thrusts slowly at first, giving her time to adjust to him and set the pace.

She was so hungry for him, she didn't want it slow.

She wanted him hard and fast.

She thrust her hips upward and held on to him tightly. She let her arms glide up and down his strong back and pulled him to her. He picked up on her need and picked up the pace. His moved his hips with a speed that would have stunned her if she weren't as determined to try out her own speed.

"Roll over. Let me ride," she demanded.

He grinned and flipped over, not breaking his stride. They remained connected and all she had to do was start her up-and-down spirals as she took control of their pleasure. She rocked and bounced and rolled her hips to a melody she swore only she could hear. But if that were the case he wouldn't have been moving with her, caressing her and swaying with her to the same sweet beat.

His upward strokes met her downward thrusts, and it was only a matter of time before she felt herself coming undone. The tingling in her thighs followed by the amazing shock wave coursing through her body soon gave way to a release so all-encompassing it made her body shake as if she were going through convulsions. He waited for her to calm down before he flipped her onto her back and took over again.

This time, his thrusts were fast and aimed at one purpose, making her come and finally giving in to his own release.

It didn't take long before they were both crying out. And the kiss that Troy planted on her lips let her know that they were far from done.

Chapter 8

"Just the way players play, all day every day…"
                                    —Notorious B.I.G.

Monday morning's staff meeting brought the reality back into Troy and Jazz's situation. The loving playfulness they had experienced that weekend had to find a way to survive given the fact that they were competing for the same job. And the uneasy collegial relationship they were slowly developing as cohosts of *Detroit Live* had to find a way to coexist with the burgeoning emotional and passionate feelings they were having as man and wife.

Troy hated meetings, any meetings. He just

wanted to be in the thick of things, doing his show and interacting with the viewers. He supposed meetings served some purpose, he just didn't think they were a productive use of his time.

He stopped thumbing through a magazine and thumping out a beat on the table with his thumb when his father cleared his throat. Troy glanced up to find Jordan Singleton, the production team for Detroit Live and Jasmine all staring at him.

He closed the magazine and stared back.

"Well?" Jordan seemed like he was waiting for some kind of response from Troy.

But for the life of him, Troy couldn't figure out what. So he just owned it. "Well, what?"

Jordan let out an exasperated sigh and threw up his hands.

The show's head producer, Carmen, took that as her cue to chime in. "What do you think about us sending Jazz to Trinidad for Carnival in a couple of weeks so that she can get some footage to air when we air your footage from the Barbados Jazz festival? We think it'll be great. The Carnival climaxes on Monday, February fifteenth and Tuesday the sixteenth, and we think it will be a real treat for our viewers. We can have an island-themed show sometime in late February where we get some up-and-coming reggae artists to come and perform and show the clips and maybe even get the proprietor of that hot new Caribbean restaurant to come and do a cooking demo with you guys—"

"Carnival could be cool. How long will we get to stay?" Troy asked. He had to cut Carmen off because if given half a chance she would have gone on and on and on.

"You're not going. Jazz is. We already have your footage from Barbados. We need something similar for Jazz. Especially if the viewers are going to be asked to pick the best of the two of you," Jordan offered in his hard-as-nails brook-no-argument tone.

Troy looked over at Jasmine. He thought about the last time he'd celebrated Carnival season in Trinidad. An overwhelming sense of possessiveness swept over him unlike anything he'd ever experienced in his life and before he knew it he had uttered the word *no*.

"No?" Jordan questioned as he squinted his eyes incredulously.

No was a word his father seldom heard, and Troy seemed to be the only person willing to say it to him on a regular basis.

"No!" Jasmine's neck swiveled so quickly as she turned toward Troy, she could have probably given Linda Blair's performance in *The Exorcist* a run for its money.

"No," Carmen whined, clearly upset about the

fact that all of her grand plans for a Caribbean-themed show might not come to fruition.

"No," Troy repeated. "I'm not going to have my wife out there with all those wild and crazy guys looking for women to prey on. It's a meat market."

"I told you that your marriage *cannot* get in the way of the show. I like Carmen's idea and Jazz is on board. So you are going to have to just get on board, too." Jordan spoke with an air of finality. "Now, as you all know, we have a poll going on our website where viewers can vote for their favorite host. So far, son, you are in the lead by three percent of the vote. After a week of you two being cohosts, we've seen a lot of traffic to the website and a lot of voting. It's interesting that you're only in the lead by such a small margin since you are the host the viewers know and are used to. It looks like it's going to be a tight race, guys."

Troy glared at his father and then turned to find Jasmine glaring at him. He wondered if she was glaring because he was in the lead or because he didn't want her to go to Carnival.

Carmen cleared her throat. "This weekend, you guys are going to be special judges for the big winter step show at Western Michigan University in Kalamazoo."

"Kalamazoo? That's a real place?" Jasmine asked.

"Yes, it is." Carmen feigned outrage. "I'm an

alum of Western Michigan University and I had some of the best times of my life in Kalamazoo. Anyway, since *Detroit Live* is popular all over the state and spreading across the Midwest and beyond, judging by the viewings on our website, YouTube and Hulu, we think it's time to start branching out beyond the Detroit area when we cover local events. We already cover a lot of national and international events. But we have been slow on moving beyond Detroit when it comes to the local. Plus, both of you guys are members of Black Greek organizations and that's a huge audience demographic. The step show is on Saturday. The two of you can go down Friday after taping and check out some of the happenings in Kalamazoo."

Troy chuckled. "Are there things happening in Kalamazoo?"

Carmen cut her eyes hard enough to slice him, but other than that, she didn't even acknowledge that he had said anything. "We'll be sending two camera guys in case the two of you want to branch out and cover different things…" Carmen's voice went on and on, and Troy stopped listening after a while.

He thought about Carmen and frowned. She'd been acting a little weird ever since he and Jazz showed up and announced they were married. Carmen had been his last big mistake three years ago when she first came on as assistant to the former producer of the show. She was cute and perky and had a figure that made a man more than pause. So, even though he had a rule about not dating women that he couldn't make clean breaks from, a rule that had kept him away from Jasmine for ten years, he had slipped and dated Carmen a few times only to find that the sizzle wasn't there. So he ended it on the best terms he could. Things had been awkward for a while, but they soon got back on track. Now they seemed to be going back to that awkward space. He just hoped that Jasmine didn't pick up on it. He decided to place Carmen in the back of his mind where she belonged.

He had more important things to think about, like why was he losing player points because he couldn't seem to stop tripping over Jasmine going to Trinidad…

It was all Jazz could do to tape the show and remain professional. If it weren't for the fact that Troy was ahead of her by three percent of the poll, she would've swapped her sweet and charming persona for her sista-with-attitude persona a long time ago. Instead her jaw hurt because she had smiled her way through the meeting and had her grin game-tight during the taping of the show.

But now that she was riding home for the day and sitting next to the man who had worked her one last good nerve, her face was on permanent grunt.

She counted to ten a couple of times, because she didn't want to just rip into him. He had been a good friend to her and was turning out to be such a wonderful lover that she went to bed with a big old satisfied smile on her face just about every night. And for the most part he was even making her rethink her former stance on marriage and husbands. The past few weeks he had been a wonderful husband-lover-friend.

But his behavior at the meeting this morning couldn't get a pass.

She turned and watched him as he looked straight ahead and navigated his SUV down the highway. She counted to ten again.

"I'm sorry. I was out of line this morning. I don't know what came over me." Troy spoke those words and the wind went out of her anger with a squish as if someone had just popped a balloon.

"What?" *Stunned* didn't even begin to describe how she felt at that moment.

She had nursed her anger all day and she was ready to tell him all about himself and how he was not the boss of her and didn't have a right to mess around with her career.

And he had just busted her bubble with an apology?

Oh. Hell. No.

The more she thought about it, the more her anger

started to build back up. Now her anger wasn't a balloon full of hot air waiting to be released. Instead she was feeling more like the kid holding the balloon that some jerk just popped for no reason. And she was pissed.

He chanced a glance at her before turning his attention back to the road. "I'm sorry. I've had a chance to think about it and I know I was wrong. I hope you can forgive me. I don't want things to get weird between us. Things were going good, right?"

She turned away from him and started looking out the window. It was dark out already and the only thing she could really see was the lights on the cars passing them and in front of them. She couldn't really make out the colors or makes, but she needed something else to focus on.

"Yes. Things were going good. And I want things to continue to go good between us. But they won't if you ever trip like you did today, Troy. You had no right to do that. I'm trying to be professional and make the best of this situation. If you win back the solo host slot on *Detroit Live*, I'm going to have to get another job. I need to leave this one in strong standing. The taping at Carnival in Trinidad could be a really good thing for me. This is my career we're talking about. No matter what happens, you're covered. You'll either be the solo host or you'll be on the business end with your father learning the ropes. If I lose, I have to find another gig."

She glanced at him and saw that he was frowning.

"If you lose, you'll still have a job, Jasmine. I'll make my father find something for you with Singleton Communication. Plus, cohosting with you isn't as bad as I thought it was going to be…" He trailed off and went silent.

"Yeah, but you still want your show back all to yourself. And I don't blame you. I've wanted my own show ever since I realized that I wanted to major in broadcast communication when I was in college. I've wanted to be the next Oprah for a long time. I may not get *Detroit Live,* but I'm going to leave Detroit with enough great segments and tapes to get a solo gig."

He didn't say anything, but at least he appeared to be thinking about what she'd said as he drove.

He pulled into the driveway and turned to her just as she was opening the door to get out.

"You have every right to be irritated with me, disgusted with me even… However you want to feel is well within your rights. I know I was out of line. And even now as I'm trying to apologize to you, a part of me, for some reason, doesn't want you going to Trinidad without me. It took me by surprise, because this is the first time I've ever felt anything this close to possessive about a woman.

"You make me feel things I'm not used to feeling for women who aren't blood related. Protective. Possessive. All kinds of things… And because it's new to me, I might mess up a little—"

She twisted her lips to the side and gave him the look.

"Okay, a lot. I'm going to mess up a lot and I might blow it big-time every now and then. But I hope we can talk about it and get back on the right track when it happens. And I'll extend you the same courtesy."

Shocked, she sputtered, "Me? I won't need it. I won't trip like you did."

He chuckled. "Yeah. Let's hope it stays that way. I'd hate to have to remind you of this moment when you do." He stuck out his hand. "Truce?"

She shook his hand. "Truce." She thought about Trinidad and how ridiculous the argument was in the first place. "And you know, there's nothing stopping you from joining me in Trinidad the weekend before we start taping for Carnival. You can certainly make it back to Detroit in time for Monday's taping if we leave right after we tape on Friday and spend Friday and Saturday and part of Sunday together in tropical paradise…"

She looked at him, and his gaze held that devilish spark she'd come to associate only with him.

He leaned over and brushed his sweet lips across her forehead in a way that never ceased to give her sexy chills.

"Actually, I'm thinking they can show reruns and I'll join you for the entire time. When you're taping, I'll get lost. When you're not, we can have some fun in the island sun, together."

She smiled.

He was probably going to find a way to do that anyway, no matter how much he had apologized.

He'd played her well.

She mentally marked this round in his favor.

"So, you know what I'm about to ask, because all the ladies want to know…" Jazz smiled at the hot R&B singer she and Troy were interviewing and the little cutie who went by the stage name Deuce Songz smiled back at her.

They were on the interview section of the set. The set had a huge dark brown sectional and several Afrocentric throw pillows. The entire vibe of *Detroit Live's* set was a celebration of black culture from the history and heritage to the music and flair.

"Is there a special lady in your life? Are you dating? Single? Inquiring minds want to know…" Jazz knew she was usually really good at getting people to open up and tell her all their business.

There had been rumors of Deuce Songz dating another artist, an up-and-coming female rapper with a pedigree that included a super-producer father and a mother who was a former rapper herself. An up-and-coming female rapper that they were all very close to because her father had dated Alicia before Alicia realized she loved Darren…

If Jazz could get Deuce to admit that he and the nineteen-year-old Kayla Kay were an item it would be a huge scoop. Of course it meant that Kayla's father, super-producer Flex Towns, might kill Deuce, but she couldn't worry about small things like that.

"Is there a special lady in my life?" Deuce pretended to consider her question. He leaned in closer. "There could be. Would you like to help me with that?"

Troy chuckled. "Okay, back up, young blood. She's taken." He wrapped his arm around her and gave Deuce a mock-stern look. "And stop trying to pin the man down, Jasmine. He's twenty-two and way too young to be thinking about settling down."

Deuce smiled and eyed Jasmine appreciatively. "I don't know, man. If it's the right woman—"

"Like I said," Troy deadpanned, "taken."

Jazz laughed. Even though she knew she looked good in the burgundy full-body catsuit and the equally fierce thigh-high burgundy leather boots she was wearing, she knew her thirty-year-old self wasn't really tempting the twenty-something crooner.

She playfully wiggled away from Troy. "Anyway, enough with the I-am-man-making-my-claim caveman routine." She gave Troy a quick peck on the cheek.

"Now back to you, Deuce. There have been rumors of you and a certain hip-hop heiress heating up the town while she's in college and starting her own rap career. Care to comment?"

Deuce narrowed his eyes. "Actually, I don't like to talk about my personal relationships. I don't like to have people all in my business."

Troy nodded. "More like you don't want Flex Towns to get all up in that—"

Jazz nudged Troy with her elbow and cut him off. "So, Deuce, tell us about the new album. Which producers did you work with on this one? Any guest appearances?"

"Yeah, the new album is the hotness! I got all the hottest producers on there. T-Pain, Timberland, Swizz Beatz, Diddy, even the boy Kanye West hooked up a track and got on the track with me. I don't have a lot of guest appearances this time. Just Kanye on his track and T-Pain got the hook on auto-tune for his track. And Kayla Kay blessed my next single with a tight sixteen bars."

"Kayla Kay, huh? She's popping up on mixtapes everywhere nowadays. What's she like? I've only seen her a few times when she attended different industry events with her parents." Jazz had actually met Kayla several times at various events that Alicia and Darren had held, so she really didn't need to ask Deuce for any information about her. She was just trying to get him to talk.

"She seems like she has a level head on her shoulders. I mean she's essentially hip-hop royalty with parents like Flex Towns and Sweet Dee…" Jazz let her words trail off, thinking maybe she could get Deuce to give her the scoop on him and Kayla after all.

Deuce gave his sexy little trademark grin. "She a nice girl, real sweet girl."

"So what was it like working with Kanye? Any temper tantrums in the studio?" Troy cut in before she could ask her followup question about Kayla.

She kept a smile on her face even though she wanted to wring Troy's neck. Cohosting sucked for that reason. Sharing the space meant she didn't always get to take things where she wanted to take them.

Deuce laughed. "Kanye is cool. He's the number-one creative genius of our times."

Troy laughed, too. "Yeah, according to him." Then he turned to the camera in mock seriousness. "But you know we love you here, Kanye. And your genius is welcomed here at *Detroit Live* anytime." He turned back to Deuce. "So you're going to stick around and perform your number-one single for us, right?"

"Of course. Of course." Deuce shook Troy's hand and gave Jazz a hug.

"We have to go to commercial right now, but when we come back, Deuce Songz will perform 'Who You With?' And he might even have a surprise guest," Troy said.

Jazz perked up. Deuce would be singing the song from his latest album that he did with Kayla. She wondered if Kayla was the surprise guest.

And she wondered why no one had told her. The producers were good for keeping little surprises from the hosts because they thought it helped get a more sincere reaction from them. But she wouldn't have wasted so much time grilling Deuce during the pre-interview and would have grilled them both after they performed if she'd known that Kayla was going to be there, too.

"Hey, Hubby, who's performing with Deuce?" she asked Troy after Deuce made his way backstage to get ready.

"It's a surprise. I don't know. Carmen just said

that Deuce had a surprise guest who would be coming out during his performance.

"Do you think it's Kayla? Did Alicia or Darren say that Flex and Deidre mentioned anything about Kayla being in town to perform with Deuce? Alicia didn't mention it to me."

"Trust me, if it is Kayla, Flex and Sweet Dee have no idea. Last I heard they didn't even want her rapping or pursuing a career until after she finished college, and it's just her second year. She's been doing the underground mix-tape scene and keeping a low profile while she defies their wishes. But her doing that track with Deuce is going to change all that. And if she and Deuce are dating…" Troy shook his head in mock sympathy. "Flex is going to kill somebody."

"And our show is going to be a part of it." Jazz almost jumped up and down with glee. "Hey, do you think that we'll have time after he performs to question both of them? At least talk to Kayla a little? I think I could make her crack for sure."

"There won't be time. And maybe that's a good thing." Troy nodded at Carmen, who was counting off to let them know that they were about to come back from the commercial break.

"Welcome back, Detroit, to where we keep it all the way live. Taking us home today is Deuce Songz performing his new single, 'Who You With?'"

The curtain opened and Deuce and his band started singing the upbeat love song about love blossoming between two people no matter what life threw at them. The beat and the lyrics showcased the sweet, fresh and new feelings that went along with young love. It was a real feel-good song, and Jazz knew Deuce had another hit on his hands. And when super-producer Flex Towns's college student/ up-and-coming-rapper daughter took to the stage, Jazz knew the scandal of those two really being involved was enough to push that song all the way to number one.

Kayla Towns—also known as Kayla Kay—came out rapping her hook and strutted across the stage and around Deuce like she was a seasoned artist. And Deuce couldn't take his eyes off her. Even if he wouldn't give a straight answer to Jazz's probing, it was clear there was more going on there than met the eye. The chemistry between the two of them was palpable.

While she swayed to the rhythm and tried to figure out how she could get them to fess up on camera, Troy pulled her into his arms and they moved together to the beat. Tingles coursed through her body, and for a minute she forgot all about everything but how it felt to be in his arms, to be one with him.

Deuce started singing again after Kayla finished

her rap. But Kayla didn't leave the stage. She stayed out there and swayed to the beat and Deuce's smooth vocal stylings.

Once they noticed Carmen giving them the wrap-it-up signal, Troy started his signature sign-off. "So, Detroit, this is your boy Troy signing off—"

"And this is your girl Jazz, and we want you to remember to keep it fresh, keep it funky and keep it all the way live! See you tomorrow, Detroit! Stay peace." Jazz chimed in and finished their goodbyes, all the while moving in time with the music and her man.

As soon as the camera light went off, Jazz broke free of Troy and went directly over to the stage.

"Kayla, do your parents know you're here instead of in class on the University of Michigan's campus?" Jazz put her hands on her hips in a mock scolding manner. Jazz had known the super-producer Flex Towns ever since she was in college and he'd dated her best friend, Alicia, for a while. That was before he found out he had a preteen daughter and reconciled with the true love of his life, former rapper Deidre "Sweet Dee" James. Since it was Alicia's big mouth that told Flex to watch the television program that outed Deidre and her secret love child, the couple made Alicia and Darren the godparents to their second child, Kayla's little brother.

"Hey, Jazz." Kayla hugged her and then she

hugged Troy. "I was hoping we could just keep this our little secret. I mean it's not like Mom and Dad can pick up the show in Minneapolis. And it probably won't be picked up by any of the bigger media networks."

"Hey, I'll have you know that our show is reaching further and further across the Midwest," Troy said with mock sternness.

"And today's show might have been picked up in some national outlets if I had gotten your boyfriend to admit on air that the two of you are an item," Jazz teased.

Kayla laughed. "I was watching that back in the green room. I don't know where you guys get this crazy information."

"It's not that crazy. And you need to be more careful, young lady. If you really don't want your parents to know, rapping on Deuce's album was probably not a good move. The song is hot and it's going to be a hit. Your parents are about to find out." All the playful sternness in Troy's voice had been replaced with the real thing. "And when they find out that you've been globetrotting around the country with Deuce instead of taking your behind to class—"

"Is everything okay?" Concerned, Deuce came over and put his arm around Kayla.

"Everything is fine. We're friends of Kayla's

parents and just making sure her head is still on her shoulders tight." Troy barely spared Deuce a glance and kept his eyes pinned on Kayla.

Jazz had to admit she kind of liked the protective stance in Troy. It made her imagine what he'd be like with any daughter they might have. And then she wondered why the heck she was wondering about that when they would probably only be married for two years tops…

"Okay, well, I guess that's my cue to make it back to Ann Arbor…" Kayla backed away. "It was good seeing you guys again. Tell Alicia and Darren I'll try and stop by in a few weeks to see the new baby. And please tell Alicia not to tell my dad that I was on the show." Kayla got a deer-caught-in-the-headlights expression and shook her head. "Although if Alicia watched, I'm sure she's already telling my father as we speak."

As if on cue, Kayla's cell phone started ringing. She looked at it. "Great, it's my dad!" She didn't answer it and it stopped. As soon as it stopped it started ringing again. She looked at it again. "Great, it's my mom!"

"I'll give you a ride back to Ann Arbor, since we sent the car for you today," Deuce said. He looked like he wanted to wrap Kayla in his arms, but he refrained from doing so.

Kayla put her phone in her pocket and smiled

at Deuce. "Cool. Can't worry about my parents' reaction now. What's done is done."

The two lovebirds barely waved goodbye to Troy and Jazz as they walked off together.

"Oh, to be young and foolish and in love…" Jazz said as she shook her head.

"Yeah. Must be nice," Troy agreed as he pulled her close. "Must be nice."

Chapter 9

Most Valuable Player

The drive down I-94 West from Detroit to Kalamazoo was about two and a half hours. They could have taken a short plane ride and then rented a car. But Troy wanted to spend the time one-on-one driving down with Jasmine. He was finding that he wanted to spend more and more time with her, even though they worked together all day and spent their evenings together at home.

His father had let them know before they left to judge the step show at Western Michigan University that Jasmine was now four percent ahead of him in the polls. At first he let the information get to him. And they'd spent the first half of the ride to Kalamazoo in silence.

They had developed a somewhat easy flow of conversation when they started talking about things they both liked: music, movies, plays, art and the like. As long as they kept the conversation away from work, the stupid contest his father had started or anything even remotely involved with it, they were fine.

"So do you miss Boston?"

"Kinda sorta… I grew up there and spent my entire life there except for the time when I was born until I was around two and then when I went to Mount Holyoke for college. I'll always love Beantown."

Troy nodded. "Hopefully you're falling a little bit in love with Motown."

"Yes, but I've always loved Detroit. From the first time I visited when I was in Alicia's wedding I've loved it. I remember looking out of the car window when you picked me up from the airport and feeling like, I don't know, this sense of rightness, you know. I always feel at home here, too. That's why I was so glad when your father—" She cut herself off as if she didn't want to ruin the mood.

"When my father offered you the job." He finished her sentence.

"Yeah," she offered hesitantly.

He just nodded and let it go. The last thing he wanted to talk about was the job. "So, I figured we could check out the hip-hop show they're having on campus tonight to kick off their weekend. They have several new underground and local artists opening up for Drake."

"Yeah, he's been heralded the second coming of Kanye West, or Kanye without all the drama and theatrics."

"We'll see. The last time I saw him perform he just stood there rapping. He didn't have any stage presence. No swagger. No umph."

"Yeah, I know what you mean. He's kind of low-energy. So, if the show is wack, I'm sure we can find other things to do…"

He chanced a glance at her to see if her "other things" was anything like what he had in mind. She licked her lips and winked at him.

He smiled.

He didn't know what he was going to do when she got her inheritance and wanted to end things. She had somehow managed to work her way into his system, and he couldn't imagine what it would be like not having her around.

He liked being married.

He liked being married to Jasmine.

Go figure…

* * *

It didn't seem like Troy wanted to talk about what might happen if she was offered the solo host position and he wasn't. And she could understand why.

After all, she was still trying to wrap her head around the fact that she was slowly developing feelings for him and he should have been her biggest rival at the moment.

"Are you sorry we got married?" *Way to go, Jazz! Go from one awkward conversation to another.*

He was silent for several long moments, and her heart started to pound so erratically that she felt like she could hear it.

"Honestly?"

"No, I want you to lie to me," she quipped sarcastically. "Of course honestly. I mean, given everything that we have going on with you know…everything. Do you regret being my knight in shining armor? Do you wish you had left my ass in the Barbados airport and gone on about your business?"

"No. I don't regret marrying you." He gave her a quick glance that held so much heat that in that brief moment she felt it overcoming her body.

He sighed. "The only thing I regret is that we did it for all the wrong reasons and put too many limits on it before it even had a chance. Because I honestly think I could probably stay married to you for more than a couple of years. And I keep having these wickedly intense desires to see you pregnant with my child. If you weren't the girl who worked my last nerve for the past ten years and was currently trying to steal my show, you would probably be the perfect wife for me."

Would probably be the perfect wife…

How did she even begin to tell him that there was no probably in it for her? He was the closest thing to a perfect husband as she would ever get. She knew that now deep in her bones. But she couldn't tell him that. Because she wasn't what he really wanted. And clearly he was counting the days until the two years were up.

She swallowed back all of the things she wanted to say to him. "You know, we haven't been using any protection, and I'm not on the Pill or anything, so you just might get your wish of seeing me pregnant with your child."

She could feel him staring at her and she turned around. "Eyes on the road."

"Sorry. I just… You know, I just assumed… Wow."

"Yeah, I think each time we got so caught up. And then there's the fact that we are married. So… yeah… How would you feel about that? You know… if I were…"

"Pregnant?" He let out a slow whistle. "I think

that would be great. When you think about it, neither one of us will probably get married again. And I've always wanted kids. I just never saw myself settling down. If you were to have my child, that would probably make me the happiest man in the world."

"Happy enough to give me *Detroit Live?*" she joked.

He laughed. "Would you be happy to give me *Detroit Live* if I did happen to give you a child and you're pregnant right now?"

"I don't know. I guess we'd have to see." She touched her stomach.

There was a time in the not-so-distant past when she would have had a panic attack at the thought of possibly being pregnant.

She smiled. She didn't feel any of the anxiety. In fact, she felt a longing so intense it made her chest ache.

"Do you want to start using protection?" Troy's voice cut through the longing she felt.

She let the question hang in the air for a minute. Nothing would have made her happier than to be pregnant with his child, other than being pregnant and being in a real marriage with him as a husband who loved her.

She shook her head. "No." *I want you to be the father of my child or children, if I ever have any.*

He nodded.

When he pulled up to the Radisson Plaza Hotel at Kalamazoo Center, they had the valet park the car and let the bellhop handle their luggage while they checked in.

Jazz wasn't any more certain about where they stood in terms of their growing feelings than she had been when they left Detroit two and a half hours ago, but she figured she'd let the heavy conversations rest for the weekend at least.

"Dang, Troy, your frat brothers are doing bad! I've never seen Kappas dropping canes like this before. And that one keeps dropping his on the most basic of steps. It's not like he's trying to catch one or throw one." Jasmine looked a little bit too happy about his fraternity brothers' glaring missteps.

They were sitting just off-stage in the big Miller Auditorium on Western Michigan's campus with two other judges. Carmen had sent one camera guy down for the day taping the step show so that they could show some clips on *Detroit Live* next week.

"So, your sorors weren't all that great."

"They worked those canes better than your boys are working them right now," Jasmine said, laughing.

He had to admit that when the Deltas did their little tribute to all the fraternities and did each frat's signature step, they were really good with the Kappa canes.

He gave her a mock frown. "Stop interrupting me. I'm trying to pay attention. Unlike some people, I take my judging duties seriously."

"Yeah, whatever, since the Kappas are the last frat to step and the sororities already went, I'm pretty sure you can stop paying attention now. The Kappas certainly aren't in the running."

"I'm keeping hope alive," Troy deadpanned.

"Yeah, you do that. In the meantime, I think I'm going to start filling out my score sheets. I know who is in *last* place." She cut her eyes at the cane-dropping Kappas.

Troy shook his head. "You're supposed to be unbiased, Jasmine."

"I am. It's going to kill me to rank your frat brothers dead last, because you know I love me some Nupes." She winked at him for emphasis. "But alas, this step team sucks to the highest of *suctivity* and I must do what I've been charged to do." She placed her hand over her forehead and feigned distress. "And just to be sure that I'm not being biased in my thinking that the Deltas killed it in this step show, I'm going to deduct three points, my line number, from their final score."

"Oh, three entire points, what a handicap…" he drawled sarcastically.

"You know, you're right. I shouldn't be so harsh

on the sorors for being the best. I'll only deduct two points."

The Kappas finally did a party stroll off the stage to Soulja Boy's song "Pretty Boy Swag." And if Troy had been inclined to throw a few extra pity points their way, they killed the inclination with their song choice. Like many true old-school hip-hop heads, Troy couldn't stand Soulja Boy.

Once he, Jasmine and the other two judges, a man who was a member of Omega Psi Phi fraternity and a woman who was a member of Zeta Phi Beta sorority, counted up the final tallies, they had a first- and second-place winner for the sororities and the fraternities. His frat brothers didn't place. But Jasmine's sorority sisters took second place, losing out to the ladies of Alpha Kappa Alpha by one point.

As they drove back to the hotel, he couldn't help but clown Jasmine. "I bet you wish you'd kept that two points in there now, don't you?"

"Not funny," she retorted as she playfully glared at him.

He laughed. "It is absolutely the funniest thing I have ever had the pleasure of seeing in my entire life. If you could have seen your face when they read the winners and the scores. It was cracked and on the ground."

"On the ground? Oh well, I guess it felt like it

had to keep your frat brothers' canes company." She smirked.

"Oh. You got jokes."

"Jokes a plenty, Hubaroni. Jokes a plenty."

"Aww, back to the nicknames again. Just when I was starting to miss them… You do care…" He placed his hand over his chest and gave her his best interpretation of lovesick and googoo-eyed.

She busted out laughing then and cracked up until they made it back to the hotel. Every time she would try and get control of herself, stop and look at him, he would turn and give her the lovesick googoo-eyed expression again and she cracked up again. By the time they got out of the car, she was holding her stomach with one hand and wiping the laugh tears from her face with the other.

"Stop. Please stop, Troy. You're killing me. I can't laugh anymore. It hurts." She panted the words out between giggles and guffaws.

He placed his arm around her and a tingling sensation traveled through his body and smack dab into the middle of his heart. He paused for a moment, getting used to the feeling.

It felt good. Even if he wasn't ready to admit it to her yet, it felt damn good.

After waking up in Troy's strong arms and having him make love to her before they got up and got ready for work, Jazz almost dreaded the

Monday-morning planning meeting with the show's producers and Troy's father.

She just hoped there wasn't a repeat of last week's meeting, where the tension between Troy and Jordan became so incredibly unbearable and Troy had gotten all bent out of shape about her going to Trinidad for Carnival.

The tension of the contest Jordan had cooked up only seemed to be held at bay when they were alone at home or in front of the camera doing the show. There was something about the chemistry she felt when she was in his arms that translated just perfectly to their connection on *Detroit Live*.

She was becoming more and more attuned to Troy Singleton, and she didn't know if that was a good or bad thing.

"So, we told you guys before you left on Friday, Jasmine was in the lead after last week's shows. But after tallying the votes that came in this weekend, you guys are actually tied." Jordan nodded at Carmen, who took that as her cue to jump in.

"Feedback has been coming in also. Viewers have written the show and expressed how much they like seeing you two together." Carmen paused and looked like she was gritting her teeth.

Jazz wondered what that was about.

"Of course there were a few viewers, mostly female, who wrote in complaining that they want the show back with just Troy as host. And complaining about his new marital status." Carmen shook her head and shot Troy a scathing look. "But for the most part everyone who has taken the time to write in seems to love the addition of Jazz, and they love the two of you together."

Jazz chanced a glance at Troy. He had his hands tented in front of his face and seemed like he was in deep concentration. His father, Jordan, had his hands folded the exact same way and had the same contemplative expression on his face.

Carmen cleared her throat in a way that made Jazz think it was some kind of nervous tic. "The viewers really loved the shows where you two did some kind of dancing together like last Wednesday when we had Cali Swag District on and you both were learning how to do the Dougie and Troy wasn't as quick picking it up as Jazz."

Jazz giggled as she remembered how funny her tall, hunky husband had looked trying to do the dance. It probably hadn't been fair for her to challenge him to a battle to see who could learn it the fastest, since she had already known how to do it. But she hadn't been able to help it.

She glanced up and saw that everyone was watching her. "Sorry. But you guys have to admit, that was hilarious."

Carmen rolled her eyes. "Anyway, the ratings are

still high and climbing. This week will hopefully be just as high. It will be interesting to see how they compare to the shows we shoot with just Troy while Jazz is in Trinidad next week. Who knew it was going to be such a neck-and-neck battle."

"Who knew indeed," Troy said as he pinned his stare on Jazz.

Jazz shrugged. "I certainly didn't. I didn't even know there was going to be a battle. I assumed I was coming to cohost a show." She gave Jordan a penetrating stare that broke him out of his contemplation.

"Well, it looks like I knew it was going to be a success, and I was right. We've already picked up another sponsor. I got the call this morning. You two just keep making that magic, and may the best person win. All right, get to work, everyone."

Jazz sighed. She couldn't wait until the camera started rolling and they started taping the show. The tension would dissipate then. And then by the time they made the drive home and walked into the house, the tension would be put to bed until they had to do it all over again in the morning. At least she hoped that would continue. More than anything, she hoped the relationship that was slowing budding and unfolding between the two of them could survive the contest that would leave one of their careers derailed.

* * *

"Dad, can I talk to you for a moment?" Troy walked up to his father as everyone else left the conference room. He caught Jasmine giving him a suspicious glance as she left the room.

"What is it, Troy?" Jordan asked as he arched his eyebrow slightly. "I hope this isn't more complaints about the contest. I've made up my mind, and we are going to see this thing through. Now, I am sorry that you're battling your wife for this position. I really like Jazz and I'm happy to have her in the family. But I'm not changing my mind."

Troy rolled his eyes. "I'm not asking you to change your mind about the contest. I want you to change your mind about me being able to go with Jasmine to Trinidad. I understand that she should tape the Carnival footage on her own. But I don't understand why she and I can't just prerecord a couple of shows to air next Monday, Tuesday and Wednesday while we're in Trinidad. Because she had to rush here for her new job and I had to get back to work, we didn't really get a chance to have a honeymoon or anything like that. And we're still in that newlywed stage. I just don't want to be away from my wife so early in our marriage." Troy couldn't believe that he was actually telling the truth. He really didn't want him and Jasmine to be apart.

Jordan gave him a piercing and penetrating stare.

"I'm running a business here, son. Something you would know about if you would stop playing around and let me show you the ropes. I'm not getting any younger, and someone has to take up the reins when I'm gone. Your sister doesn't want anything to do with the company. She's too busy being a wife and mother and spending Kendrick's money like your mother spent mine. And now you're in here talking about honeymoons?" Jordan shook his head and heaved a heavy sigh laced with a small dose of contempt.

"If I weren't your father would you even be coming to me with this kind of request?"

Troy narrowed his eyes. "No. If you weren't my father, I wouldn't be standing here at all, let alone trying get your permission to go to Trinidad with my wife. If you weren't my father, I would have left *Detroit Live,* hired an agent and found another gig long before this contest nonsense. I've done nothing but show my loyalty to the Singleton Communication and *Detroit Live.* Maybe I'm not doing it exactly like you want me to… But I'm my own man, and the sooner you get that, the smoother things will go between us. I want to go to Trinidad with Jasmine. Can you work with me to make that happen?"

Jordan looked at him with an expression that bordered on respect. Or at least as close to respect as Troy had ever seen from the man.

"You really love Jazz, don't you?"

Troy nodded. "Yes. Yes I do."

Jordan smiled. "Well…I'll be… All right, fine. Carmen is going to have a fit, because she has the shows booked already. And she's still pissed about that stunt you pulled taking off to Barbados in the first place and messing up a week's worth of lineups. And I'm not even going to get into whatever little thing the two of you had going on a few years back. You really could have handled that a lot better, son—"

The last thing Troy wanted to get into was his mistake with Carmen. So he cut his father off instead.

"It really is for the best, Dad. If I do two shows on my own while Jazz is away, that might give me an unfair advantage in your little contest and give me more face time with the viewers. Viewers who were already mine to begin with…" Troy couldn't believe he was actually giving up such an advantage and felt a shock course through him as the words fell out of his mouth.

Jordan must have been shocked, too, because his eyes widened and his mouth fell open. "Well, I'll be…you really do love Jazz. I never thought I'd see the day when my son would grow up and fall in love. Fine. I'll handle things and try to smooth things over with Carmen. You can go with Jazz to Trinidad next week. In fact, you two can take the entire week as a honeymoon gift from me. Now get to work while you still have a show to host."

Troy smirked. "Thanks, Dad! I appreciate it." He left the room before Jordan changed his mind.

Chapter 10

Playing for keeps…

Trinidad and Tobago had to be two of the most beautiful islands in the world. Clear blue sky and an even clearer, almost majestically royal blue sea made it so that a person could barely tell where one stopped and the other began. The islands were so lush and green, with flora and fauna in abundance as far as the eyes could see. And the natural beauty of the land didn't have anything on the beauty of the people.

Like many islands in the Caribbean, Trinidad and Tobago boasted a healthy mix of people and cultures. With folks from a variety of ethnicities, from African descent, Chinese descent, South Asian descent, Middle Eastern and European all proudly claiming the same heritage: Trinidadian! The people in all their variety were just as beautiful and diverse as the islands. And seeing the costumes and finery associated with Carnival during the weekend and the two-day Monday and Tuesday climax of the event in the parades, the dancing in the streets and nonstop partying offered even more excitement for the eyes.

Jazz was very pleased with the interviews she had done and the footage she had been able to shoot. She'd even gotten a chance to hang out with her husband a little during downtime. And now they were spending the rest of the week on the much quieter and serene island of Tobago for a short honeymoon.

She had no idea how Troy had managed to talk his father into giving them the entire week off to spend in this island paradise. But she wasn't even going to question it.

All she knew was she wanted to make the most of the time they had away from worrying about who was going to be the solo host of *Detroit Live*. She wanted to spend the time in Tobago making love to her husband on a secluded beach or walking hand in hand as their toes sank into the sand. All she wanted was memories to last her when it was all over and they went their separate ways.

The Plantation Beach Villas where they were staying in Tobago were neatly nestled in a plush hillside that overlooked the most amazing white-sand beaches and aqua-blue waters. In addition to the tropical, almost rain forest-like flora and fauna, palm trees seemed to enclose the tranquil space, almost keeping it a secret, a hidden gem. The villas themselves were the cutest shade of peach and white and were classic turn-of-the-twentieth-century West Indian gingerbread architecture. Each two-story villa had three full bedrooms, including a master suite, a fully equipped kitchen and a living room.

After a day of snorkeling, they had dinner brought to their villa from the hotel restaurant and were enjoying a light dessert of tropical fruits on the private balcony just off the master bedroom.

The fruit platter had an assortment of starfruit, mango, cherries, dates, guava, papaya and chunks of fresh coconut. And they took pleasure in feeding each other from the bountiful tray.

She opened her mouth as Troy held out a piece of mango for her and gingerly sucked the sweet juice from his fingers as she took the fruit.

"Mmm…" She closed her eyes and leaned back into his arms. "This is probably the best vacation I've ever had. I see why people get married! Honeymoons are *so-oo* worth all the I-do-till-death-do-us-part stuff."

She picked up a chunk of coconut and traced his lips with it before placing it in his mouth. He chewed it and then leaned in for a kiss.

His strong, penetrating lips caressed her mouth slowly, and the delicious fruit they had both eaten tasted even sweeter laced with their combined desire. They allowed the kiss to linger, tongues circling and spiraling around and around in their combined mouths.

He moaned.

She sighed.

He lifted her onto his lap and the kiss became more demanding. Their hands joined in, groping, clutching and feeling their way home. His strong fingers grazed her nipples, which were already at attention.

She reluctantly pulled away from the kiss for a moment and stared into his penetrating gaze.

"Have I thanked you for getting your father to let us have this time off for a honeymoon?"

"You have. But you can always thank me again, and again and again." He winked and gave her a slow peck on the lips.

"Don't worry. I will." She traced his mouth with her tongue, slowly savoring the taste of him and the fruit.

"Do you feel guilty about what we're doing to our friends and family? Lying to them about being married—"

"We are married. We're not lying."

"I know we're married. I mean *really* married and in love like everyone thinks we are?"

He shook his head. "That's between us, and it's none of their business. I don't feel bad about anything we've shared, Jasmine. Not one bit of it."

He looked so intense and sincere that if she were a more trusting person that would have been the moment she would have let all of her guards down. But she wasn't. This marriage had an expiration date, and she needed to remember that.

"Did I ever thank you for coming to my rescue and marrying me?" She gave him another quick peck on the lips.

"You have." He kissed her long and sweet. "But." He kissed her again, his tongue diving into her mouth with purpose and promise. "If you want to thank me again… I can think of lots of ways…" He traced her kiss-swollen lips with his thumb. "You don't have to thank me for any of this, Jasmine. I'm probably getting more out of this than you are."

"Well, I don't know about that, Hubster, I'm getting great sex, a new BFF, a big inheritance… And did I mention the great sex?"

Troy laughed. "You might have mentioned

something like that. I'm more interested in this new BFF thing. Is Alicia going to hunt me down and take me out because of my new title?"

"No, she's still my BFF. I just have two of you now. But…" She dropped her voice to a whisper. "I'll let you in on a secret… You're my favorite BFF."

He pursed his lips in mock consideration. "This wouldn't have anything to do with the great sex thing, would it?"

She clutched her chest and opened her mouth in mock horror. "Why, never would we give in to our baser instincts. It was the knight-in-shining-armor-aiding-a-damsel-in-distress move that put you over the top. The great sex was just a bonus." She broke into a laugh.

He cracked up, too, but turned serious as he moved her from his lap to the seat and stretched her out in front of him. He slid off her underwear, all the while staring deeply into her eyes.

"I think it's bonus time. What do you think?" he asked.

"I think it's always time for a bonus," she responded as she opened her legs a little wider.

He smiled and then looked over at the fruit platter. "You know, I really didn't care for this fruit much."

Fruit? You have me laying here all splayed out and you're talking about fruit?

Jazz took a deep breath and forced a grin. "I couldn't tell. You sure ate your fair share of it. I should know. I fed it to you."

He rubbed his hand across his chin, still looking at the fruit. "I know. But it just wasn't sweet enough. It could've been sweeter." He picked up a piece of papaya and turned to look at her finally.

The devilish gleam in his eyes gave everything away.

But when he ran the papaya over her slick, exposed folds and then popped the fruit in his mouth there was no question. He clearly never wanted her to look at fruit the same way again…*ever*.

He picked up a piece of mango. The ripe fruit and his very capable fingers penetrated her, working her until she gave him more of the sweetness he desired. When he removed the mango, it was coated in her juices. He licked the fruit lovingly before eating it.

"Now this is what I'm talking about. This is what sweet tastes like." His hooded eyes captured hers and her heart rate quickened. "I would share. But this sweetness is only for me. You don't mind, do you?"

She wanted to say, *hell no! Eat until you get a cavity, until you get the sugar, as the old folks say.*

But instead she just smiled and shook her head. "The fruit was sweet enough for me. Now I'm kind of craving something salty. I think I know just where to find it later…" She let her words trail off suggestively.

He helped himself to a little more fruit laced with her, and then he stopped and kneeled in front of her, placing one of her legs over each of his shoulders. "Too much fruit, not enough sweet," was all he said before he began giving her the most intimate of kisses. He lapped and tugged and nipped and soothed, using his mouth, tongue and lips to cause an eruption so fierce she felt like she had been run over by a truck by the time she stopped shaking and screaming.

She really hoped that the hyped selling points of it being a "secluded and private villa" were true. Because if they weren't, then the villas around them were getting an earful. Luckily, the balcony was private enough, and she didn't have to worry about anyone seeing her stretched out, being pleasured, whipping her head back and forth and speaking in tongues.

He continued lapping greedily until she stopped moving and didn't think she had another ounce to give. He stood up and reached for her hand, leading her over to the balcony rail.

Just as he was about to position her in front of it and lean her over, she stopped and turned to face him. "I think you're forgetting my craving for something salty, Hubby."

She dropped to her knees, keeping her eyes up and focused on him. She unzipped his shorts and released his sex from the flap in his boxer briefs.

She ran her tongue across the head and moaned. "Mmmm, salty with just a hint of sweet." She covered him with her mouth, sucking him in and working her jaws into a sweet, suctioning caress. She let her hand hold and stroke the parts of him that she couldn't reach with her mouth.

He slowly moved his hips back and forth. His hands moved to her hair and he gripped it, lightly nudging her in time with his own movements.

She kept her eyes on him, loving his intense reaction to her. He threw his head back and groaned.

"Oh, God! You're killing me, girl."

Since her mouth was busy she couldn't respond or even smile, really. But she could giggle inside and revel in how wonderful it felt to make her man— even if he was only temporarily so—feel good.

She let him fall out of her mouth with a pop and teasingly licked up and down his shaft. "Say my name."

She kept her eyes on him, letting him know that he would only get teasing until he complied.

He gave her a hooded gaze and seemed to shudder

with anticipation each time her tongue flicks connected. "Jasmine."

She moved away after giving him a small peck on the tip. "Unh, unh, unh. That's not the name that's going to bring you to ecstasy. Jasmine would never! But Jazz…" She winked at him.

He groaned. "Come on, Jasmine, baby, please."

She shook her head. "Say my name, Hubster. You can do it."

He grinned. "You're killing me."

"Ahh, but what a sweet way to go…"

"Okay, Jazz…" He moved his hips forward slightly and she took him in her mouth again just as he finished with, "Mine."

She could have stopped and teased him some more, but she knew that was the closest she would probably get to him calling her Jazz. He thought he was so clever, and she fully intended to make him suffer later. But at that moment, all she wanted to do was taste.

So she swirled her tongue around him as she worked her jaws and lips with one purpose only— pleasing her husband.

The nature of their marriage, how long it would last, how much she was starting to fall in love, none of that mattered. Just when she started to feel his knees buckling in the sweetest release, he pulled away.

"I want to be inside of you when I come." He

pulled her up and finished what he'd started earlier, draping her over the balcony rail.

He stepped behind her, lifting the skirt of her little lounging dress and spreading her legs so that he could stand between them. He entered her in one solid thrust, pushing all the way to the hilt.

She gasped at the fullness but pushed all the way back wanting more. Luckily they were only two stories up. Not that it mattered. She couldn't be distracted by seemingly trivial things like how far up they were and if the railing was really as sturdy as it felt.

The only thing she could focus on was how good it felt to have him inside of her, thrusting and retreating at a pace and speed that pushed her closer and closer to the edge of what promised to be the most earth-shattering orgasm of her life.

When his arms reached around her and squeezed her breasts as he used his hold to lift her slightly and pull her away from the railing and even closer to him, she lost it. She panted and stuttered out an incoherent scream as her orgasm ripped through her. Troy soon followed with a long groan and his own release.

Just as she was about to slump over and rest for a while, she felt herself being lifted and carried inside.

Troy finished undressing her and then undressed

himself before he cradled her in his arms in bed. They both let out satisfied sighs and she dipped her head to his chest to inhale the pure unadulterated masculinity of him.

"My Jazz. Mine." He mumbled in a slurred sleepy speech tone. "I'm keeping you, girl. You're mine."

Her heart stopped and restarted at a breakneck pace. Was it the great sex talking, or did he really mean he wanted to keep her? And if he did want to keep her, for how long…

She really hoped he meant to keep her forever, because that's how long she was starting to realize she wanted to keep him.

After spending the last day of their honeymoon in Tobago hiking in the Western Hemisphere's oldest protected rain forest and exploring the sights, Troy and Jasmine capped off their stay by taking part in the local entertainment of goat and crab races. Watching the crab race was so much fun they almost regretted eating the winning crab when it was all over. *Almost…*

As they walked down the secluded beach hand in hand, Troy almost wished they had another week to spend there. The honeymoon had put so many things in perspective for him, and he had come to realize so many things about his lovely wife.

"This has been so amazing. I almost don't want to go home. It's so relaxing here." She glanced at him and tilted her head saucily. "And then there's you…"

"Yeah? What about me?"

"I don't know. It's like… Well, I'm going to just keep it real with you. Being with you these past few weeks has been amazing. And I just can't believe that it's so amazing and I…" Her voiced trailed off and he wondered what she would have said next.

He wondered if he even dared to hear what she was going to say or dared to have any kind of hopes or expectations about it.

They walked in silence for a little while longer, letting the soft island breeze take away any anxiety or stress they might have had about returning to the contest at work and the battle between them.

"Can I ask you a question?" She stopped walking.

"Sure." He took a seat in the sand and pulled her down onto his lap. He kissed her lips softly, letting his tongue trace and mark its path before it dived in.

She kissed him back for several minutes before putting her hand on his chest and pulling away. "Why didn't you want a cohost for *Detroit Live?* I think the past few weeks we've been really good together."

"Don't. Let's not go there, Jasmine. We're having a good time. It's our honeymoon and I really don't want to spend our last night on the island on that topic. We'll be back in the thick of things soon enough when we get back home."

She narrowed her eyes and glared at him. "Maybe we should just get a divorce now and I can just find another job then." She made to get up and he pulled her back down.

"What do you mean get a divorce? If you get a divorce then your mother's money will go to your father. I thought you didn't want that. I thought you would be brave enough to at least stick it out six months so that some of the money could go to the charity for single mothers... What's your problem?"

"My problem is you. This." She waved her arms, gesturing back and forth between herself and him. "This marriage. The contest. All of it. I didn't know when I signed the contract with your dad that he would make us battle for the solo host position. I thought at most I'd be your cohost, charged with bringing new energy to the show. I knew you'd hate it, and I have to admit when I signed the contract that was one of the perks, that you would *absolutely* hate it and having me as a cohost would work your nerves. But I figured we could use that energy to make magic on the screen.

"And then I ran into you in that airport and you literally saved me. You wrapped me in your arms and you saved me—" She stopped and took a deep breath.

"Then why do you want a divorce? Why do you want to leave me?" He had to fill the silence even though he was almost afraid to hear her answers.

The passion in her voice, her tone, everything, had his chest feeling raw and exposed. He probably shouldn't have asked her any questions. Because if she kept talking, God knew how he would deal with it.

She closed her eyes and laid her head on his chest.

He let out a breath of relief. If she didn't say anything else, he might have a chance to keep his barriers up. He might be able to continue giving only as much of himself as would allow him to still feel safe from the floodgate of emotions that threatened to burst any minute.

Then he heard her soft voice mumble, "I'm scared. I think I'm falling in love with you," and he knew he was done for.

He kissed her soundly, penetrating her mouth in an effort to forestall any more confessions. The barriers he had that were meant to help him keep his distance and keep it together when she left in six months or two years had broken down and he was exposed and too open for his own comfort. So he kissed her, trying to fill back up.

Soon she was ripping his shirt off and her hands trailed his chest, leaving sexy little goose bumps in their path.

"You are going to have to buy me some new shirts when you get this inheritance of yours, Jasmine. And you will get your inheritance because I'm not giving you a divorce now."

Not now. Not ever.

She planted soft pecking kisses down his chest. "You're rich." Peck. "You can afford to sacrifice a few shirts for the cause." Peck.

He relished her touch and felt himself bulging and coming to life each time her hand caressed and each time her lips connected with his chest.

"What cause?"

"The cause of wild and passionate lovemaking, Hubinator."

"Oh, my favorite cause, I try to donate often…" he said as he fell backward onto the sand.

She smiled, but it didn't seem to reach her eyes. She laid her body on top of his and kissed him again. As they kissed, their hips ground against one another, and before he knew it she had released his sex from his pants, maneuvered her thong to the side and enveloped him in the soft, wet heat of her womanhood.

She looked deep in his eyes as she worked her

hips up and down slowly. He kept her gaze, knowing that he never wanted to look anywhere else.

The silence of the moment spoke volumes, at least to him. He saw forever in her eyes. Love was all over her face, and he wondered if he was imagining it. He knew what he was feeling besides the bliss of her winds and dips and suctions. He was feeling his heart swell up with a fullness that could only be until-the-end-of-time love.

He wished he could tell her. But if she was going to divorce him in six months or two years then he couldn't. He couldn't open himself up to that kind of pain.

So he pulled her face closer to his own instead and kissed her with everything inside of him. He wanted her to feel all the love he had inside.

She kissed him back with so much passion it literally stole his breath. He gasped and clutched her to him as he lifted his hips from the sand and thrust upward in a ferocious heat.

He had to say something.

"I don't want you to leave me, Jasmine. Please don't leave me, baby." The words ripped from his mouth before he could censor himself.

She groaned. "I won't. I can't. I'll stay as long as…" She threw her head back and let out a low-pitched moan as an orgasm took her over.

Her sex clenched down on his so tightly and so

quickly it caught him off guard. Before he knew it he was grabbing her buttocks and holding her still as he spilled his seed inside of her.

They rode out the waves of their climaxes together, and it was only after they had gotten back to their villa that he realized she had never finished. She had never told him what he had to do so that she would stay with him forever.

Chapter 11

Game. Set. Match.

Jazz sat in her dressing room fuming.

The honeymoon was over. And back in the real world Troy and Jazz worked every day remembering the pact that they had made in Tobago. They were playing to win and in it together. However, after the show that day, Jazz was finding it hard to remember that pact.

The knock on her dressing room door started out as just a tap. Just one tap that apparently was supposed to make her jump up and let whoever it was in. But she knew who it was and he could keep on knocking, but he couldn't come in. Only Troy would assume that he could just tap on the door once and be welcomed with open arms.

One week he was up in the ratings. The next week she was up in the ratings. The following week they were tied. If they were horses racing they would have been neck and neck. It was starting to take a toll on their marriage and the tenuous bonds they were starting to build.

Today they taped their Caribbean special and showed clips of Troy in Barbados at the Jazz Festival and Jazz in Trinidad at Carnival. They had even been able to get reggae artists Gyptian, Cham and Junior Reid all to perform. And because the audience seemed to love when she and Troy danced or had some kind of sparring, they had a battle to see who was best at doing old-school reggae dances. They challenged each other to see who was best at the Pepper Seed, the Bogle, the Butterfly and the Dutty Whine.

Of course, given Jazz's Bajan roots, she assumed she would be the winner, but Troy gave her a run for her money. She won. But it was close. The reggae artists all performed solo and were set to close out the show after Jazz and Troy did a Caribbean cooking segment with the owner of a new Caribbean restaurant downtown.

Jazz didn't intend to participate as much. Besides

the fact that she was already a pretty accomplished cook, she had a public motto that cooking was overrated to uphold, after all. She'd told Carmen that and tried to beg off the demo, but the woman wouldn't hear of it.

So there she was standing on the stage with Troy and Gina Langston pretending to learn how to make a curry chicken roti.

She must not have been paying enough attention for the arrogant Gina, because Jazz heard a slight annoyed tone in the beautiful Jamaican woman's voice as she asked her to pass the onions.

Troy passed the onions instead and rolled his eyes. "My wife thinks that cooking is overrated, so she's not really into the demo, Gina."

"Well, if she plans to remain the wife, she better learn how to cook or she'll lose you to a woman who can feed you in more ways than one." Gina drawled her words out in a sweet and sexy slight Jamaican accent.

Jazz felt her eye twitch and her head did a full swivel as her arms folded across her chest. The in-house audience picked up on the tension immediately because the ohhhs and ahhs and laughter were almost instantaneous.

She willed herself to remain quiet. Because she was not going to give Little Miss Jamaica a trip to Barbados...at least not on the air.

Troy and Gina finished the demo, and Jazz did well not to snatch Gina bald when the hussy actually fed Troy a piece of roti.

Troy laughed and looked at Jazz. "See, that's how you treat a man."

The audience erupted and they went to commercial.

Jazz glared at Troy as he continued to make nice with their "guest." Jazz couldn't be that fake. So she went over to stand by the producers instead.

"He's such an asshole. I knew this might be a problem when I booked Gina. He has such a roaming eye. One woman will never be enough for him. I certainly learned the hard way." Carmen's soft voice whispered angrily behind her. "She's just his type, too. Well, more the type he used to date, not the type he married."

Jazz spun around. *First Troy with the insults and now this chick?* "What?"

Carmen backed up. "Don't shoot the messenger. I'm on your side. I want to see you get your own show. I'm the one who talked Jordan into looking for a new host and getting Troy into the office. I couldn't believe that the two of you had gotten married. I was only trying to save you from the heartache I suffered, like *so* many women in the long line of broken hearts that that asshole leaves in his wake. Gina will probably be next after you." Carmen's eyes had an evil, bitter glint. "You need to go back onstage for the closing."

Stunned, Jazz didn't know how she managed to close the show and smile. But the smile died as soon as the camera light went off. She glared at Troy and tried to formulate what she would say to him, but she couldn't think of a thing. So she walked off instead.

The knocking grew progressively louder and she rolled her eyes and decided to take off her makeup instead of responding in any way.

"Open the door, Jasmine. Please." Troy's calm, matter-of-fact voice after he'd made a fool of her on national television and in front of all their friends and coworkers for the past few weeks grated on her nerves.

"Go away, Troy. Please."

"What happened? We were having a great show and you got all weird at the end. What did I do?"

She got up and unlocked and opened the door. No need to give them even more stuff to talk about. "Tell me about Carmen."

She realized that her eyes were glossed with unshed tears but she didn't care at that point. The hurt needed someplace to go, and if it took crying, no matter what her mother had drilled into her about never showing weakness in public, she was going to let them flow.

Troy walked into her dressing room. She closed the door and followed him.

"Carmen says Gina is just your type. *Way* more your type than I am... And apparently way more your type than Carmen was. How could you have me up in here not knowing that you had had a relationship with Carmen? You left me wide open for that foul chick to throw it in my face. You were supposed to do me better than that..."

She sat down on the sofa and he sat down next to her.

"It was nothing to tell. I dated her three years ago when she first came to the show as assistant producer. The chemistry was lacking and I moved on. She didn't stand a chance because I had already lost my heart to you years ago, Jasmine. No other woman had ever stood a chance after I picked you up from that airport and kissed you in that restaurant. It wasn't fair to Carmen and it wasn't fair to the other women, either. I should have been man enough to just risk my heart with you.

"I am man enough now. I'm ready to put it all on the line. I love you and if you ever left me it would kill me. I don't want this marriage to end, ever. I want us to be together until we are old and gray. And I want to share children and grandchildren and great-grandchildren with you and only you. You are the only type I have, Jasmine. You. Only you. I love you."

Jazz felt the tears running down her face. He was saying everything she wanted to hear. Finally. Could she trust it? She wanted to.

She looked at him. He was so solemn and serious. She rolled her eyes as she wiped away her tears. "You really need to get over yourself, Hubby. It's not that deep. We love each other and we'll stay married until the end, until one of us takes their last breath. So what? Big deal…there's no need to be so-oo melodramatic."

He sighed. "Be serious, Jasmine. I love it that you joke and you're playful and you're always pushing my buttons. But I need to know that you are for real. That finally this, us, this marriage can be for real."

She nodded and let go of the knot in her chest and throat. "It's real, Troy. It's as real as it gets. I love you. I probably always have." She smirked. "I love yuh mad. I love yuh bad. I love yuh so much dat if yuh ever let another woman feed yuh roti or any such ting again you and she gwan havta deal with me, nuh? And you ain' gwan like what I do to yuh!"

He laughed and kissed her. "I'm counting on that, Jasmine. I'm betting my entire life on it."

Chapter 12

"Don't wanna be a player no more..."
                                        —Big Pun and Joe

After some time...

After Jordan's six-month contest was over, Troy and Jasmine walked into the recently renovated studio of *Living with Troy and Jazz* and were shocked when all of their family, friends and coworkers jumped out and screamed, "Surprise!"

They hadn't been expecting a surprise party, much less a surprise party that doubled as a celebration of their new syndicated show and the wedding reception they'd never had. Carmen had left *Detroit Live* soon after the Caribbean show debacle, and Jordan made them play the contest out until the bitter end to announce a winner. They had actually tied in the end, and it was clear that everyone loved the two of them together.

The happiness and joy of everyone around them couldn't hold a candle to the happiness and joy in their hearts.

"So, Dad, are you going to be able to hold off a few more years for me to join you in the office?" Troy joked with Jordan as he, Jasmine, Darren and Alicia all stood around talking.

"I think I can manage awhile longer, especially now that you and Jazz are going to be giving me another grandchild. Between your sister's kids and the grands you'll be giving me, I'm sure one of them will want to take over Singleton Communication one day. I suppose I'll have to hang around long enough to watch them all grow up so I can train them."

Alicia laughed. "Well, I can tell you now that Kendrick and my father have dibs on Sonya and Kendrick's brood for Taylor Publishing. So you better get these two to give you lots of grandchildren, Jordan."

Jordan laughed as well. "We'll see, Alicia. We'll see. I like a good contest, and going up against

Taylor Publishing for a heir might just be the kind of excitement I need to keep me going."

Jasmine held their goddaughter, Ashley, who had grown a lot and was getting to be very active. She amused herself by grabbing Jasmine's earrings, pulling on Jasmine's hair and balling her little hand into a fist and sucking on her knuckles.

"I can't believe the two of you are going to have a nationally syndicated talk and variety show. I always knew you were nosy enough and ran your mouth enough to give Oprah a run for her money." Darren playfully teased Jasmine and Jasmine just ignored him and continued focusing on little Ashley.

Alicia shook her head. "No, I always knew that Troy's inquisitive twenty-questions-asking behind would make a great talk show host. When I first started dating you, that boy used to get all up in my business."

Troy rolled his eyes at Alicia's memory of when she and Darren had first started dating. "You know I had to make sure you were going to do right by my boy. I had to get all in your business, just in case."

"Yeah, whatever," Alicia said.

"And I'm sure Troy's harmless questions had nothing on the third degree Jazz put me through. She got everything but my social security number." Darren feigned indignation.

Jasmine shook her head and laughingly blew

raspberries on Ashley's little cheeks. Troy watched her and knew he couldn't wait until she gave birth to their child. He looked at her small baby bump and glee threatened to overwhelm him, so much so that he felt it in the middle of his throat.

Words could never express how happy Jasmine Stewart-Singleton had made him.

"Well, it's my turn to ask the questions now," Alicia said, moving into her role as editor-in-chief of Taylor Publishing's *Black Life Today*. "Did you know that the two of you would be able to make magic once you stopped fighting, or rather fighting your attraction and giving love a try? Not to mention you started out as a married couple battling for the same job and now you're about to have your own nationally syndicated show. Did you ever dream it could happen? That it was even possible?"

Jasmine looked at him and she got that playful, devilish gleam in her eyes that he was starting to really love.

"You know, Alicia, I'll tell you like I told him. I knew I could do for him what Martin did for the people. You know everyone talks all that stuff about it being a man's world. But us women? We keep the tempo. Basically, it just reached a point where I had to say, baby, let me upgrade you. You need me. You need a real woman in your life. People go their entire lives trying to find their equal. With my hustle and his hustle, I could totally upgrade him." She winked at him and then continued playing with Ashley.

No, this woman is not remixing Beyoncé lyrics up in here!

He shook his head and rolled his eyes, because apparently he was the only one who'd picked up on Jazz's inside joke. It was their own little couple thing and he liked it. He liked having a *couple thing!*

"What about you, Troy? Did you ever imagine all this could happen?"

He nodded. "Right…you know…at first I didn't know. But it didn't take me long to see that even though I'm a movement by myself, together we could be a force. Me plus Jasmine just equals better math. I'm a good look, but she is definitely my better half. And even though I'm hot, together we burn it up. So yeah, I kind of knew she'd make me better."

Jasmine rolled her eyes as she giggled and shook her head. The look in her eyes said he'd got her with his remix on the Fabolous and Ne-Yo lyrics. She gave Ashley one last kiss on the cheek and handed her to Alicia.

"Okay, folks, the hubby and I have to make our rounds and thank everyone for this surprise party." Jasmine placed her hand in his, and it felt like home. "We'll connect with you guys later, girlfriend. Because you know I haven't gotten my fill of my goddaughter, not to mention the boys."

"Yes, make your rounds and remember you guys owe your first interview to me and *Black Life Today*. And don't think that little song lyrics thing y'all do is going to work. I want a serious, hard-cutting, in-depth—"

"Baby, let them go and greet their guests." Darren took their daughter from Alicia's arms, placed his arms around his wife and walked her away.

Alicia was still mumbling questions as her husband pulled her away.

"You two go on and make your rounds. Remember, tomorrow it's back to work. I expect you two to be syndicated all over the world by next year." Jordan winked at them as he walked away.

Jasmine wrapped her arms around Troy and tilted her head. He bent down and gave her a peck on the lips.

She grinned. "Fabolous? Seriously? That's what gave it away. You know Alicia is a hip-hop head from way back. Now she's on to us."

Troy laughed. "Umm…Beyoncé and Jay-Z? I think you're the one who gave it away. Who wouldn't recognize 'Upgrade U' when they hear it?"

"I was very clever with mine. She wouldn't have caught it."

"I think the only reason why she didn't catch it that day in the hospital when Ashley was born was because she had just gone through labor. But I don't think my dad or Darren picked up at all. It can still be our thing, Jazz *Mine*." He kissed her deeply.

"Mmm…. It could totally be our thing." She smiled. "I like having a thing with you."

"And I love having a thing with you."

"We're going to make it, huh?"

"Shit, yeah, we are. I always knew we would, once you stopped playing."

"Once I stopped playing. Please, this coming from the man who said they'd have to pry his player card out of his cold dead fingers." She smirked. "Did you really know? How did you know? You didn't know…"

"I knew. I knew it at first kiss."

"At first kiss? Which first kiss? Our wedding? Ten years ago? When? When did you know?"

He kissed her. "All of the above. I knew it every time I kissed you. I know it every time I kiss you. And every kiss is like the first kiss."

"You're slick. I like that. I guess I'll keep you."

"Oh, you'll keep me, huh." He chuckled. He'd like to see her try to get rid of him.

"Yeah. Because I knew from the first time you kissed me that you were the one. I just had to give you time to mature and catch up to my swagger." She laughed and pulled away.

He pulled her back and wrapped his arm around her shoulder as they walked off to greet the rest of their guests. He had to smile, because he knew life with Jasmine would probably never be dull and they would always keep one another on their toes. Marriage didn't mean playtime was over. It meant the fun was just starting. And he couldn't wait to play with the woman he was born to play with for the rest of his life.

Epilogue

"I'm the original playa from the Himalayas!"
—Martin Lawrence's Jerome

Jordan Singleton stood at the Barbados cemetery and placed a huge bouquet of colorful roses on Carlyne Stewart's grave.

"Well, sweetheart, our plan worked. Maybe not exactly the way we thought it would work… But it worked. We thought me hiring Jazz, having her and Troy work together, and you putting that marriage clause in your will would have made them come to fall in love and get married."

He chuckled as he thought about how crazy he'd thought Carlyne's plan was. He hadn't thought it would work at all. He knew his son and he didn't think the man would ever settle down.

But Jordan absolutely adored Carlyne and he couldn't deny her anything, especially not when she got the news that her cancer had come back and it was terminal. He and Carlyne had developed a close friendship through the years after he met her at one of the Whitmans' functions. He would have done anything for her, including put up the money to orchestrate the trickiest matchmaking plot ever.

And it actually worked… Two old players got the best of the youngsters without anyone being the wiser.

"They did things a little backward, Carlyne. They got married and then they fell in love. But they ended up right where we wanted them. And they are going to give us a grandbaby soon. I wish you could be here to see your first grandchild. But something tells me you're looking down from heaven."

He wiped away a tear and his voice choked. "*Detroit Live* has been picked up for syndication and is now *Living with Troy and Jazz.* Our kids are about to be parents and they are about to be stars. Jazz decided to put the inheritance in a trust fund for the baby and any other children she and Troy might have. So I guess I have to say it because I know you're waiting for it. You were right. Jasmine and Troy are perfect for one another."

He turned and walked away.

* * * * *

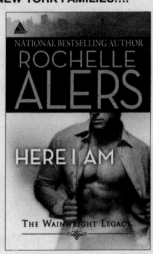

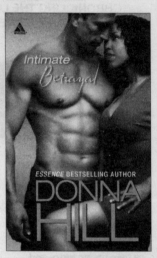

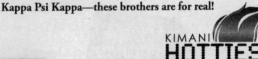

Wilde IN WYOMING *Saddle Up...to a Wilde*

Kimberly Kaye Terry

invites you to discover
the Wilde brothers of Wyoming

Book #1
TO TEMPT A WILDE
On Sale February 22, 2011

Book #2
TO LOVE A WILDE
On Sale March 29, 2011

Book #3
TO DESIRE A WILDE
On Sale April 26, 2011

REQUEST YOUR FREE BOOKS!

2 FREE NOVELS
PLUS 2 FREE GIFTS!

KIMANI ROMANCE™

Love's ultimate destination!

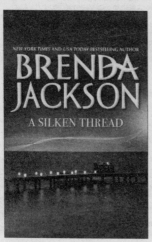